EV

Conners spent a moment looking from Kimble to Donnelly, as if sizing them up in some way.

"Now as I understand it," Conners began, "you boys have been asking a few questions about Susie Washburn."

"That's right," Kimble confirmed.

"Not to step on anybody's toes, you understand, but around here a man's business is considered his own," Conners stated. "It's a private thing and should stay that way. You agree?"

"Yes," Kimble said, "but–"

"Now, now, now," Conners interjected. "No 'buts.' You agreed with me."

As he spoke, a large black beetle somehow found its way onto the table and began to waddle slowly across it. Conners slowly drew a stately Bowie knife out of his boot, all the while watching the insect.

"Now, seeing as these things you're asking about are of a personal nature," Conners went on, "I'd advise you to quit while you're ahead. Everyone's got their place in the world, and stepping into someone else's spot just throws everything out of whack. Only trouble can come of dipping your bucket in another man's well. A fella could get hurt."

Quick as a flash, Conners struck with the knife, impaling the beetle on the tip of his blade, where it struggled in vain.

"A man who does that is like a bug scampering into the light," the deputy continued. "He's asking to get stepped on."

As he finished speaking, Conners placed the tip of his knife under the heel of his boot and pressed down, crushing the beetle as he drew the knife back.

He then looked from Kimble to Donnelly, before uttering, "Understand?"

EVANGELINE

EVANGELINE

By

Herc Samson

EVANGELINE

This book is published by HS Impavid Publishing.

ISBN: 978-1-937666-98-9

Printed in the U.S.A.

ACKNOWLEDGMENTS

I would like to thank the following for their help with this book: GOD, who has continually blessed me without measure; my loving and supportive family; and readers, who have far too kind with their praise of my work.

Thank you for purchasing this book! If, after reading, you find that you enjoyed it, please feel free to leave a review on the site from which it was purchased.

Also, if you would like to be notified when I release new books, please subscribe to my mailing list via the following link: http://eepurl.com/ginmVT

Finally, for those who may be interested, I have included my blog info:

Blog: https://hercsamsonbooks.blogspot.com/

Chapter 1

They came in the middle of the night. Susie Washburn was asleep when they arrived, peacefully snoozing and dreaming of better times. At age seventeen, she had already blossomed into a beautiful young woman, with high cheekbones, clear skin, full pouty lips and bright blue eyes.

Not far from the bed where she slept, a baby's crib resided in one corner of the room. In it lay an infant, swaddled and sleeping.

Without warning, the bedroom door flew open and a young man swiftly stepped inside carrying a rifle. He was tall and handsome, but with a mocha skin tone that stood in stark contrast to Susie's ivory complexion. He walked towards the bed, then reached down and roughly shook Susie's shoulder.

"Susie!" he uttered in a fierce whisper. "Susie, get up!"

Susie opened her eyes and yawned. "What is it, Jaspar?"

"They're here!" he replied.

Suddenly, Susie was wide awake. Now looking frightened and anxious, she practically leaped from the bed, crying, "Oh my G–"

"The baby!" Jaspar interjected, cutting her off. "Get the baby!"

Susie rushed over and gently pulled the still-sleeping baby out of the crib, keeping it covered with a blanket. As she picked the child up, she stealthily peeked out the bedroom window, which was on the second floor of the house they were in.

Outside were a bunch of men in white robes with matching hoods: Klansmen. They already had a cross burning in the yard. The leader of the Klansmen, the Grand Dragon, wore a red sash with his ensemble – a symbol of his authority and badge of office. He walked forward and began speaking.

"We know you're in there, nigger!" he shouted. "We're gonna hang your Black ass out to dry!"

This pronouncement was accompanied by whoops and shouts of support from his fellow Klan members.

Inside, Jaspar grabbed Susie's arm and pulled her away from the window, saying, "Come on, come on…" Shifting his grip to Susie's free hand, he quickly led her out of the bedroom.

All of the lights in the house were out, leaving them to find their way in the dark. Racing carefully down a nearby set of stairs, they found themselves in a large living room.

Most of the furniture was covered, a testament to the fact that the house had been uninhabited for a long time. In the center of the room was a coffee table, positioned between two couches and nestled on a large rug.

Setting the rifle down, Jaspar grabbed the end of the coffee table and pulled it to the side. He then rolled away the rug, revealing a secret door set in the wooden floor. Attached to it was a ring latch designed to lie flush with the floor. Jaspar grabbed it and started to pull.

Outside, a score of armed, robed Klansmen had surrounded the house, plainly intent on making sure no one got away. Holding a revolver, the Grand Dragon stood with his back pressed against the outer wall of the structure, next to a window.

Yelling towards the inside of the house, he bellowed, "You should have kept with your own kind, boy. Black and White don't mix. Especially not a Black man with a White woman!"

Inside, Susie – already nervous – grew more anxious after hearing the Grand Dragon's words.

"Hurry!" she urged as Jaspar struggled to lift the hidden door.

Straining with effort, Jaspar said, "I'm going...as fast...as I can."

With a mighty heave, the hidden door finally came open. There was practically no light, but they could make out a set of stairs leading down into darkness – a secret room.

"Alright, quick now," Jaspar said, motioning Susie forward.

Susie, on the verge of going down the steps, suddenly turned around and gave Jaspar a huge hug and a kiss on the cheek.

"Love you," she said as tears began falling from her eyes.

"Love you, too," he replied. "Now go."

Without another word, Susie quickly – but carefully – went down the stairs. When she reached the bottom, she took a quick glance around. It was too dark to really see anything, but she got the impression that she was in a small, enclosed space.

"Okay," Jaspar said from above her, "you remember what I told you about how to get there?"

"Yeah," Susie confirmed with a nod.

"Alright, I'll meet you there," he stated. "Just follow the breeze to get out."

The tinkle of broken glass in the kitchen drew Jaspar's attention for a moment. Their late-night visitors were obviously getting ready to storm the place.

"Shit!" Jaspar blurted out. Turning back to Susie, he said, "Remember: follow the breeze!"

He then slammed the door back down, then hurriedly put the rug and coffee table back in place before retrieving his rifle.

At that juncture, Klansmen began smashing windows all around the house. Jaspar understood that the obvious intent was to confuse him as to where they'd be coming in. Rather than try to cover all fronts, he ducked down behind one of the couches, rifle at the ready, and waited. Unsurprisingly, he didn't have to wait long.

By that time, the Grand Dragon was next to the front door. He nodded at a fellow Klansman – a big, burly fellow – who stepped forward and kicked the door in. As the door banged open, the two of them raced inside, guns blazing, but their eyes were unaccustomed to the dark of the house's interior.

Jaspar shot the first Klansman without hesitation, hitting him in the chest; the man went down and stayed still. The Grand Dragon, however – who was at the rear – dove behind some furniture at the sound of the first shot.

Hearing movement behind him, Jaspar spun to his rear, shooting. He hit two more Klansmen who had slipped in through the back door – one in the stomach and the other in the hip. Both went down screaming in pain but clearly still alive, their pretty white robes now stained with their own blood. However, they had provided enough of a distraction for the Grand Dragon, who was now behind Jaspar, to get off a shot.

The bullet struck Jaspar in the shoulder, causing him to drop his gun. Wincing, he loped towards the stairs, hoping to make it to the second floor as more Klansmen rushed inside, some carrying lamps. He was roughly halfway up the stairs when a second bullet took him in the calf, making him cry out as he went tumbling back down the steps. Almost immediately, the Klansmen began kicking him and beating him with makeshift weapons – baseball bats, tire irons, and more – all the while calling him names.

"Damn nigger!"

"Jungle bunny!"

"This'll teach you to keep away from our women!"

Down in the hidden room, light spilled in from cracks in the floor above Susie. Her tears flowed freely as she heard the awful sounds of Jaspar being battered, and she had to cover her mouth with her hand to keep from whimpering aloud. Finally – mercifully – the beating stopped.

"Alright, let's finish this outside," the Grand Dragon ordered. "You can't properly lynch a nigger inside, can you?"

Some of the Klansmen laughed at this as they dragged Jaspar, semi-conscious and breathing raggedly, out into the yard. Only the Grand Dragon and one other Klansman remained inside.

"We looked all over," the Klansman reported. "She's not here."

"What do you mean she's not here?" The Grand Dragon demanded. "She *has* to be here! She was traveling with that nigger! Where else would she go? Who the hell would take her in?"

"Look, I don't know. But dammit, she just ain't here!"

Clearly vexed, the Grand Dragon let out a yell of frustration, at the same time kicking over the coffee table.

"Something else, too," the Klansman continued. "There was a crib up there…sheets are still wet. There was a baby in there not too long ago."

At this, the Grand Dragon seemed to freeze for a moment.

"What do you want us to do?" the Klansman asked.

The Grand Dragon didn't immediately answer. Instead, he simply lowered his head, seemingly in thought.

"Hey," the Klansman muttered. "What do you want to do?"

"Find it," The Grand Dragon said solemnly. "And kill it."

Chapter 2

Still in the hidden room, Susie heard everything the two Klansmen above her were saying. Given what they had done to Jaspar, it was no revelation that these were terrible people, but what they said about the baby went beyond her ability to imagine.

Eyes wide and covering her mouth in horror, she backed towards the rear of the secret room, which – as her eyes adjusted to the dark - she now realized was little more than an underground cave.

That actually made sense. This was Louisiana, and a good chunk of the state was below sea level. That meant that building underground structures like basements weren't practical – they would flood too easily. In this instance, the original owners of the home had apparently found a natural cave on a slightly elevated piece of land and ingeniously decided to build over it. The end result was a house with a secret room that no one would ever suspect was there. How Jaspar came to be aware of it Susie didn't know, but at the moment she was just grateful that he had.

A soft breeze unexpectedly wafted from behind, blowing Susie's hair over her face. Pulling her hair back and turning around, she suddenly remembered Jaspar's words about the breeze. Looking intently at where it appeared to originate, she noticed that the breeze seemed to be coming from a nearby tunnel. Holding the baby tightly to her bosom, she boldly entered without hesitation.

The tunnel was dark and damp, but that was to be expected. Susie made her way slowly, not wanting to trip and fall with the baby in her arms. She also prayed that there was nothing dangerous in the passage. The last thing she needed was to get bitten by something like a copperhead, or brush up against some poisonous plant. That would be the end for her *and* the baby.

Thankfully, she didn't encounter anything that impeded her progress (although she did stumble once or twice). Roughly half an hour later, Susie emerged, extremely muddy, from a shallow tunnel at the edge of a swamp. Stepping out, her feet sank into the muck, but she managed to keep her balance. Holding the baby tightly, she pulled herself up and began trying to high step her way to dry land. Looking back the way she had come, she saw the house where they had stayed about a quarter-mile away, being consumed by flames.

Seeing the fate of the house – and knowing Jaspar's as well – she suddenly started crying.

"Oh, Jaspar…" she sobbed softly. "I'm so sorry."

Suddenly, the baby began crying, bringing Susie back to herself. She started trying to shush the infant while continuing across the muck until she reached solid ground. Once there, she kept moving, knowing that she and the baby were not out of danger. Stepping over a large log, she jumped back all of a sudden when it turned out to be a huge alligator that snapped at her leg.

Frightened, she backed away from the reptile, which began waddling towards her. Unexpectedly, something tried to grab her from behind. Startled, she screamed and twisted around to the rear of the thing that had accosted her. It was only then that she noticed it was one of the Klansmen. Still dressed in full Klan regalia, he turned to face her.

"Well, girlie, we've been looking all over for you," he said menacingly. "Guess you better come along with me now."

The Klansman advanced on her. Susie reached down with her free hand, picked up a large rock and held it like a weapon.

"You keep away from me and my baby," she said angrily. "Keep away or I'll brain you."

The Klansman stood still, holding out his empty hands in a non-threatening way.

"Now, hold on there, girl," the Klansman told her. "That baby's an abomination – something the good Lord never meant to be. It's a sin for it just to be alive. So why don't – Ahhh!!!"

The Klansman shrieked as the alligator suddenly attacked, locking its powerful jaws around his leg. When she had initially circled away from the man, Susie had put him between herself and the reptile, which had continued creeping forward the entire time. The Klansman had been so focused on her and the baby, he didn't even recognize the danger until it was too late.

Now with a grip on the leg of its prey, the gator yanked back hard. The Klansman fell to the ground howling and struggling to get away as the alligator began dragging him back towards the swamp. Susie stared in horror for a moment then fled through the swamp with the Klansman's screams filling her ears.

Chapter 3

The headquarters of the Federal Bureau of Investigation was a solemn structure that typically invited awe and reverence. However, FBI Special Agent Billy Kimble was typically awed by little and revered even less.

At the moment, he was approaching the desk of a Bureau secretary that was located outside a large office. He was a handsome man in his mid-thirties, with dark hair and a dazzling smile. As was typical for him, he was using that smile to full effect as he took a seat on the edge of the secretary's desk.

"Hello, Martha," he said to the secretary. "I must say, you get more beautiful every time I see you."

Martha, a gorgeous redhead, smiled at the compliment. "That's sweet of you to say, Billy, but the answer's still 'No.'"

"Well, why not for Pete's sake? What's so bad about having dinner together? I mean, do I stink or something?"

Martha appeared to ponder for a moment. "Well, now that you mention it..."

She trailed off, grinning. Kimble let out a faux groan of disappointment and stood up.

Walking towards the office behind her, he pointed at the door, asking, "Is he in?"

Martha nodded. "Yeah. He's expecting you."

Taking that as his cue, Kimble was about to go inside the office, but paused for a moment at the door. It was a standard office door, with wood paneling on the lower half and frosted glass at the top.

There was lettering on the glass, which Kimble read aloud. "David Stanford – Special Assistant to the Assistant

Director to the Executive Assistant Director to the Associate Director."

"Geez," he continued. "That far down the totem pole, you might as well just say he empties the chamber pot."

Martha snickered as Kimble, shaking his head in disdain, entered the office.

Inside, the room was large and fairly plush. At the center was a large desk, behind which sat David Stanford. He was a slim man in his early forties with thin hair and sharp, angular features.

Sitting in one of two chairs in front of the desk was a brown-haired young man that Kimble didn't know. However, judging by indicators such as his suit and shoes (which strictly adhered to Bureau protocol), he was a new agent.

Both men rose when Kimble entered. Stanford came from behind the desk with his hand extended.

"Billy," he said as the two shook hands heartily. "It's good to see you."

"You too, David," Kimble told him. "Congratulations on the promotion."

"Oh, it's nothing, really," Stanford noted. "I guess someone was just needed for the job and they pulled my number out the pot."

"Yeah, I was just telling Martha about that pot," Kimble remarked, which earned him an odd look from Stanford. However, it quickly passed as Stanford gestured towards the young man.

"Billy, I'd like to introduce you to Trevor Donnelly," he said. "Trevor, Billy Kimble."

Donnelly and Kimble shook hands and exchanged pleasantries, following which Stanford wandered back to his chair while telling his visitors, "Have a seat, both of you."

The two men obliged, at which point Kimble asked, "So what's going on?"

"*This*," Stanford replied as he pulled a large manila folder from his desk drawer.

Stanford slid the folder towards Kimble, who opened it. Inside was a picture of a pretty young woman, along with some other paperwork. Donnelly leaned over to get a look at the folder's contents as Kimble sifted through them.

"Her name's Susie Washburn," Stanford continued. "Seventeen, of Evangeline, Louisiana. Missing, possibly dead."

Kimble rubbed his chin, thinking. "Kidnapped?"

"Not likely," Stanford offered. "Her family's well-off, but nowhere near rich. Not much profit in kidnapping poor people."

"How long?" Kimble asked.

Stanford leaned back in his chair. "She's been gone about seven months–"

"Seven months?!" Donnelly interjected. "And it's just being reported?"

Stanford shrugged. "She's a runaway. She's taken off seven times in the past two years alone. But she was never gone more than a week before."

Kimble, getting annoyed at Donnelly reading over his shoulder, simply handed him the entire file.

"Well, seven months is a hell of a lot longer than one week," Kimble noted. "What took her parents so long to report it?"

"That's the funny thing: they never did," Stanford stated. "Her father didn't, anyway. Her mother died about ten years ago."

Looking at the file, Donnelly frowned. "Says here that she's been to the doctor nine times in the past two years. Fell down the stairs three times, tripped and hit her head on the coffee table twice, fell off a ladder while changing a lightbulb..."

"Can't blame her from running away from home, then," Kimble observed. "Sounds like the house was trying to kill her."

"Or someone in the household," Donnelly noted. "If I didn't know better, I'd say someone was beating her."

"No shit, Sherlock," Kimble quipped.

Donnelly, plainly agitated, was on the verge of responding but didn't get an opportunity.

"Alright, that's enough, Billy," declared Stanford. "Trevor's right: it looks like an abuse case."

"So what are you thinking," Kimble inquired, "that the father went a little overboard the last time and popped her a little too hard, then got rid of the body?"

"Possibly," Stanford conceded. "The town's right on the edge of the Louisiana swamps. Drop a body down in that muck, and odds are it'll never be found. Even if it is, there probably won't be enough left of it to identify. The gators, rats, and about a billion other animals will have fresh meat stripped down to the bone in less time that it takes to tell about it."

"What about the local sheriff?" asked Donnelly. "Didn't he investigate the situation? Or go talk to this girl's father?"

"The local sheriff *is* her father," Stanford replied, causing the two agents to look at him in surprise. "As you can see, it looks like you two really have your work cut out for you."

"Us two?" Kimble muttered, eyebrows raised in surprise. "You mean–"

"Yeah, Billy," Stanford stressed. "He's working with you. Why else did you think he was in here?"

Kimble shrugged. "Training?"

"Agent Donnelly's a fully trained agent and your partner on this," said Stanford. "You got a problem with that?"

"None at all," Kimble declared, shaking his head. "But, well," – he cast a quick glance at Donnelly – "isn't he a little green?"

"No more than you were when you first started," Stanford remarked.

"But this case looks simple enough," Kimble stressed. "I don't see the need for–"

"Don't talk about me like I'm not here!" Donnelly fiercely demanded. "I'll have you know, Agent Kimble, that I am a fully authorized and accredited agent of this organization. I went through the same training and testing as you. I didn't cut corners or have someone on the inside cut me any slack. I'm here because I earned the right to be."

Kimble, eyes wide, laid his hand effeminately across his heart and turned to Stanford. "Well hush my puppies…"

Glaring at Kimble, Donnelly stood up and angrily stalked out of the room. Kimble watched him leave and then turned back to Stanford, smiling.

"Kids these days," Kimble commented with a grin. "So sensitive and excitable. They go running off at the least little sign of adversity."

"Just don't let him run too far," Stanford advised. "He's got your tickets, and you leave in two hours."

The smile vanished form Kimble's face. He swiftly came to his feet and then went hurrying after Donnelly.

Chapter 4

Stanford had slightly exaggerated their departure time, meaning that Kimble actually had an opportunity to go home and properly pack for the trip. At present, he and Donnelly were on a plane, en route to their destination in Louisiana.

They sat on the same row, with a seat between them. Donnelly, sitting by the window, took the opportunity to read Susie Washburn's file again. Kimble, seated by the aisle, was hitting on a stewardess who laughingly rejected his advances.

"So how about it?" Kimble asked.

"It's very flattering," the stewardess admitted, "but I'm engaged."

Kimble winced and placed a hand on his chest. "Oh, you've lanced me. And through the heart."

The stewardess giggled. "I've got a funny feeling you'll survive."

She then walked away, with Kimble staring after her longingly. Donnelly looked at him in exasperation.

"Do you have to do that everywhere we go?" he demanded.

Kimble gave him a confused look. "Do what?"

"Try to pick up every woman you see."

"Pick up?" Kimble repeated, feigning shock. "Me? I was just being friendly."

"So you were just being friendly with Martha back at the office when we left?"

"Of course."

"And with the other secretaries?"

"Yes."

"And the woman at the ticket counter?"

"Well, uh…"

"And now the stewardess."

Kimble was silent for a moment. "So what's your point?"

Donnelly shook his head in disgust and went back to reading the file. As the stewardess passed by again, Kimble stopped her.

"Excuse me," he said, "I was about to take a nap and I was wondering if you could wake me up in an hour?"

The stewardess nodded. "Sure thing. I'll be happy to."

She then walked away. As she left, Kimble leaned back and crossed his arms, smiling smugly.

"Hear that?" he said to Donnelly. "She said she'd be happy to."

"Yeah, and I'm sure she will," Donnelly added. "With a bucket of cold water…"

****

The rest of the flight was uneventful, and they landed without incident. However, as they were exiting the terminal with their luggage, Kimble and Donnelly noticed a short man in a seersucker suit holding up a sign with their names on it.

"Looks like they rolled out the welcome wagon for us," Kimble stated.

With that, they approached the man in question.

"Excuse me," Kimble said, "but this is Special Agent Donnelly, and I'm Special Agent Kimble. You're expecting us?"

"Yeah," the man said, then extended a hand. "Merrill Wright, glad to meet you."

"Mr. Wright, of course," Kimble said as they each shook the man's hand in turn. "You're the sheriff of the county here."

"Parish, Agent Kimble," the sheriff corrected.

Kimble frowned. "Excuse me?"

"They don't have counties in Louisiana," Donnelly chimed in. "They have parishes. If you'd gone through that file in any detail, you'd know that."

Kimble looked as though he had a comment to make in reply, but before he could, Wright said, "Well, if you have all your luggage, we can get moving."

He then began walking away, heading for the airport exit. The two agents quickly followed, catching him in only a few steps.

"We were given your name as a contact," Kimble said to the sheriff, "but I wasn't aware that you were planning to meet us at the airport. I thought we'd come by your office after we arrived."

"Well, I figured that you boys would wanna start right away," Wright explained, "so I decided hanging around the office waiting for you would just be a waste of time. Seemed like I could meet you at the airport, and save you some time and a trip."

"How's that?" Donnelly asked as they exited the airport and headed towards a nearby parking lot.

"Well," Wright droned, "I'm supposed to be assisting you fellas with this investigation by providing a car and manpower and such. But to be frank, I'm not sure how much help I'll be."

Kimble's brow crinkled. "Why do you say that?"

"To start off with, we're a small parish," the sheriff said, "and I don't have much in the way of men or resources. Second, the place you're going to is a coupla hours up the road–"

"A couple of hours?" Donnelly repeatedly almost incredulously. "But the town's supposedly less than sixty miles away."

"That's as the crow flies," Wright said matter-of-factly. "But Evangeline is pretty much in the heart of the swamp."

At that point, they came to a halt in front of a shiny black automobile. Wright then pulled a map out of his jacket pocket and spread it out on the hood of the car as he continued talking.

Pointing to a line outlined in blue on the map, Wright relayed, "This here's the only road in or out, and it's got more curves and loops than a pretzel. They had to build it that way – had to build around the swamps, 'cause there's no way to go through them."

"And that's why a sixty-mile trip takes two or three hours," Kimble concluded. "Well, thanks for coming to meet us, Sheriff. You've saved us at least an hour, I'd say."

"Well, that's not my only reason," Wright confessed. "The sheriff down there, Washburn, he's a hard man but he's got a lot of friends in a lot of places thanks to certain 'connections' he has - Klan connections, to call a spade a spade. Even in my office. I think it might have hurt your case if we'd met where other ears could overhear things."

"Things like what?" Kimble inquired.

"Things I couldn't tell you there without getting good people in trouble," Wright said. "Things that might even get them killed."

Chapter 5

The two agents spent a moment absorbing Wright's statement. Assuming what he said was true, it would certainly affect how they went about their work.

"So why has it taken you so long to report this case?" Donnelly asked all of a sudden.

Wright gave him a hard look. "What was that?"

"You heard me," Donnelly said. "What was the delay in reporting this?"

Wright's eyes narrowed. "You trying to say that I haven't done my job?"

"No," Donnelly responded, "but I'd like to know why there hasn't been an investigation until now."

"And what the hell was there to investigate?" Wright demanded. "A girl was missing, but someone has to report it to the law to get an investigation started, and her father *is* the law. What was he gonna do, report it to himself? You young shit! You think you know everything!"

"Not everything," Donnelly shot back. "Just how to handle an investigation."

Fist balled, Wright took a menacing step towards Donnelly. Thankfully, Kimble stepped in between the two men as they closed in and pushed them away from each other.

"Stop it, both of you!" he ordered. He pointed at his partner, who was still trying to get close to Wright, and yelled, "I said back off, Trevor!"

Breathing deeply, Donnelly stopped his advance. He put his hands on his hips and turned away, kicking at a rock on the ground. Kimble turned back to Wright.

"I'm sorry for my partner's behavior," he apologized. "We really do appreciate your help. Now what were you about to tell us?"

Wright still looked angry, then let out a frustrated sigh. "It's alright. I'm a little antsy about this thing myself. What I was saying was that Washburn's got friends in a lot of places, particularly law offices, so meeting in my office wasn't really a good idea."

"You also said something about getting people in trouble?" Kimble noted.

Wright nodded. "Yes. There's a woman in Evangeline – Ginger Meadows. She's doing some things up there that, well, a lot of folks don't feel is really good for the community. She's the one who reported Susie Washburn missing to me. I've managed to keep her name off my reports, and I'd like to keep it that way. She's a good woman, and I don't want to see any more trouble come her way just for doing the right thing."

"We'll keep that in mind," Kimble assured him.

"Much obliged," Wright stated. "I really do appreciate it."

Stepping forward, Donnelly said, "Look, I didn't mean to offend by what I said before."

"No offense taken," Wright declared. "We just have to remember that we're all on the same side here. I just hope I've been of some help. She never really seemed like the bad sort, so I hope you find her okay."

"Who? Susie Washburn?" Kimble asked in surprise. "You've met her?"

"Sure," Wright replied with a nod. "I picked her up at least two of the times when she ran away. The last time, she stole a hovercraft and lit out across the swamp. That's when she almost got away."

Kimble reflected on that for a second. "She almost got away? By going across the swamp?"

"Sure," Wright answered. "That's the best way to go. It's really hard to follow someone, and there are lots of places to hide."

"Do you think she could just be hiding out in the swamp now?" inquired Donnelly.

"Not for this long," Wright stressed, shaking his head. "The swamps ain't no playground. We've got a few people, though, like Mike Trapper and old Mama Lu, who stay out there, but it takes a special kinda person to live in the swamplands. No, I doubt if she took to the swamps. Besides, no one around here's reported missing so much as an oar, let alone a boat or hovercraft."

"What about somebody walking across?" suggested Donnelly.

Wright, in process of folding the map and handing it to Kimble, looked at Donnelly in shock.

"A man would have to be crazy to even try," he insisted. "You know how many things are out there that can kill you? And I'm not just talking about the gators and such. Lots of the plants are poisonous, too. My brother-in-law went fishing for gar out there once and had some plant's sticker go through a hole in his boot and get stuck in his foot. Two days later his toes were black and big as grapefruits; they had to cut the leg off all the way up to the knee."

Donnelly looked disturbed by what he'd just heard as Wright handed Kimble a set of car keys.

"Any other cheery news we should hear about before we leave?" inquired Kimble.

"None that I can think of," Wright told him. "Oh, watch out for Sheriff Washburn. He's the law in those parts, and not a good man to be enemies with."

"Good to know," Kimble acknowledged with a nod. "Thanks."

"My pleasure," Wright attested. "Take care, gents."

He then shook their hands again and departed.

Chapter 6

Sitting behind the wheel, Donnelly drove along a twisting, winding one-lane road while Kimble slept on the front passenger side of the car, snoring softly. Donnelly gave him a look of disgust, then reached over and vigorously shook him.

"Hey – Sleeping Beauty," Donnelly said. "Wake up."

Kimble abruptly came awake. "What? What is it? Are we there yet?"

"No, we're not," his partner answered. "Look, I agreed to drive the last half of the trip because you said you wanted to have time to look at the file and get caught up on this case. Instead, the only thing you've caught since I got behind the wheel is forty winks."

Kimble yawned. "Relax, kid. You're too uptight. To be honest, though, it reminds me of *my* first time in the field: worried, tense, anxious..."

Donnelly frowned. "Who says this is my first time?"

Kimble laughed. "Oh, come off it! It's written all over your face. You're nervous, irritable, and wound up tighter than a virgin's snatch, as my old Grandpa used to say."

Donnelly cut his eyes at his partner before turning back to the road, but didn't respond.

"Besides," Kimble continued, "I've been watching you, and you do everything by the book. Stiff and strait-laced, that's you. From the way you dress to the way you carry your weapon, you're a stickler for the rules. An experienced field agent knows exactly which procedures to follow and which are only guidelines, which ones are true and which ones are bullshit. So are you still trying to say that this isn't your first field assignment?"

Donnelly stayed silent for a moment, then said, "So what if it is?"

Kimble clapped his hands and laughed heartily at his partner's admission.

"And what's wrong with how I carry my gun?" Donnelly added, glancing down to where his weapon was positioned beneath his left arm. "It's loaded and holstered just like–"

"Just like the book says," Kimble chimed in. "To be honest, nothing's wrong with it, but every agent worth a hill of beans knows that you should have your weapon in your comfort zone. Having it damn near tucked in my armpit like yours would drive me crazy, so I carry mine lower."

As evidence of this, Kimble pulled open his coat and revealed his weapon, holstered low next to his stomach.

"Also," he went on, "a lot of experienced agents like to carry a little something extra, an insurance policy, so to speak. See?"

As he finished speaking, Kimble twisted his back towards Donnelly and lifted his coat, revealing a gun tucked into his waistband at the small of his back. He then lowered his coat and turned back around.

"Is that an officially authorized weapon?" Donnelly asked.

"Nope," Kimble admitted with a smile. "But once again, that's a part of recognizing the bullshit. I can see you've got a lot to learn, kid, but not to worry. You just focus on driving, and I'll take care of the rest."

With that, Kimble put his hands behind his head and closed his eyes.

"You'll take care of the rest, huh?" Donnelly asked.

"Yep," his partner confirmed.

Without warning, Donnelly slammed on the brakes. Kimble flew forward and smacked his head on the dashboard.

"Are you crazy?!" Kimble yelled furiously. "You trying to get us killed? Why'd you stop like that?"

Donnelly, smiling, merely pointed out the windshield to something in the road ahead of them. Kimble's eyes went wide.

"Holy shit," he uttered, still staring.

Immediately ahead of them, stretching from one side of the road to the other, was an enormous alligator.

Chapter 7

The two agents simply stared at the gator for a moment. As if aware of the attention it was receiving, the reptile suddenly bellowed sonorously; the sound echoing across the swamp.

Donnelly turned to his partner. "So what does your field experience say to do about this?"

"Just run over the damn thing," Kimble suggested.

"I can't run over that. That thing probably weighs a ton."

"Then go around it."

"How? The map specifically says that we need to stay on the road until we reach Evangeline. The swamp starts just a few feet away on either side."

Kimble rubbed his forehead, where a purple bruise was starting to form.

"Shit," he muttered. "Maybe we can scare it off and–"

"*We*?" Donnelly repeated in surprise. "Where did this 'we' come from? I'm supposed to stick to driving – remember? – and let you take care of the rest."

Kimble glared at him hatefully for a moment, then scratched his temple, thinking.

"Drive forward," he said after a moment.

"I already told you we can't run over that thing," Donnelly protested.

"I'm not asking you to run over it. I just want you to get close to it."

Although he wasn't sure what his partner was up to, Donnelly complied, pulling the car up as close to the gator as possible. At that point, Kimble reached over and pressed on the car's horn. It blared loudly, making Donnelly wince.

After about ten seconds, Kimble eased up on the horn. He then rolled down his window and peeked out. From his vantage point, he could still see part of the alligator's tail, indicating that it hadn't moved.

"Dammit," Kimble muttered. He then spent a moment trying to remember what he knew about gators.

Truth be told, he had actually toured an alligator farm once when he was about ten years old. However, roughly all he remembered from that excursion were two basic facts: first – despite appearances – gators were pretty fast on land. Second, there were generally afraid of and tended to avoid humans.

"You plan on doing something about this *today*?" Donnelly asked, interrupting his thoughts.

"Patience, young man," Kimble admonished as a plan of action occurred to him.

Taking out the weapon holstered at his hip, he gently opened the passenger-side door and warily stepped out. He could still see the animal's tail as he closed the passenger door, so it hadn't gone anywhere.

Kimble hurriedly took off his suit coat, and then – to Donnelly's surprise – hopped on the hood of the car. Still holding his weapon in one hand and his coat in the other, he slid forward until he could see the reptile.

Up close, it seemed even bigger than he had assumed. It appeared to be sunning itself, and was clearly in no particular hurry to move on.

Carefully balancing himself on the hood, Kimble got on all fours. He then leaned forward over the front of the car and began using his coat to swat at the gator, hoping to shoo it away.

"Move along now," he told it, continuing to buffet the animal with his coat. "Get, damn you."

Initially, the animal seemed to pay Kimble no mind. But after about fifteen seconds, it was clearly starting to get annoyed, as evidenced by the fact that it opened its mouth and let out something akin to a hiss.

Sensing that the reptile was getting agitated (and assuming it was about to move on), Kimble redoubled his efforts. Thus, he was caught by surprise when the gator suddenly snapped its jaws viciously in his direction, banging its head on the front of the car. Kimble was so startled that he instinctively tried to scramble backwards, but somehow lost his balance and went rolling off the passenger side of the hood.

He landed on his back with a solid thud that was accompanied by a sound akin to a thunderclap. At the same time, he felt a lancing pain near his nether regions.

Kimble immediately jumped up and began fanning his blackened, smoking trousers – the result of the gun at his back going off. Simultaneously looking around for the alligator, he saw the animal – apparently startled by the gunfire – finally waddling off the road. He also saw Donnelly, inside the car and laughing hysterically.

Chapter 8

Donnelly was still driving when they finally reached the town of Evangeline. Next to him, Kimble was positioned facing backwards with his knees in the passenger seat. The seat of his trousers, blackened where the gun had gone off, faced the windshield.

Donnelly glanced at his partner with an expression of distaste. "Do I have to look at that?"

"What?" asked Kimble.

"Your ass, that's what."

"I'm sorry, okay?" Kimble apologized, "but it hurts too much to sit in the seat right now. Let's find a doctor and have him take a look at it."

"I thought you said it only grazed you?"

"It did, but that doesn't mean I'm not worried about infection," Kimble stated. "You heard Wright earlier; this swampland is crawling with disease."

As they drove through town, people began turning to look at them.

"Well, I wish you'd stop making a spectacle of yourself," Donnelly told him. "People are starting to stare. They're going to think you're a real ass."

Donnelly then chuckled mildly at his own little joke.

"Ha ha. Very funny," his partner monotoned, although he did notice people behind them staring after the car. But this was to be expected – they were strangers in a small, isolated town that probably received few visitors.

"I'm serious!" Donnelly insisted. "If we're going to get these people's cooperation, we need to be ass-cepted by them!"

Donnelly then laughed loudly at his own remark before continuing, saying, "And that's...that's...that's not gonna happen while...while they see us demonstrating any...any...any...ass-inine behavior!"

He then became practically giddy with laughter.

Meanwhile, Kimble merely shook his head in disdain. "I should have never left the farm, but noooo... I wanted to join the FBI..."

****

It wasn't hard to find the doctor's office. Like much of small-town America, Evangeline's downtown/business area consisted of just a couple of cross-streets. Thus, the two agents would have found it on their own, but asking a man on the street had saved them a few minutes.

At the moment, Kimble was lying face-down on an operating table while Dr. Reardon (as the name on the door said) – dressed in a white lab coat and with a stethoscope around his neck – put a bandage on his wound. Donnelly leaned against a nearby wall, watching.

Many folks would have been too modest to have someone else in the room while they were being treated for an injury like this. Donnelly, however, had served in the war and seen more than his fair share of action. More to the point, he had been observed by others in various states of undress while being treated for wounds far more serious than a bullet graze. In short, having Donnelly in the room didn't bother him.

As he continued his ministrations, Dr. Reardon – elderly but active – asked, "So how did this happen, again?"

"Incident with a gator," Kimble said. "But as I mentioned when we arrived, we're with the FBI. Any chance you could answer a few questions for us?"

"Sure, if I can," Reardon replied.

On cue, Donnelly took out a pad and pencil.

"How long have you been the doctor around here?" asked Kimble.

"Going on fifty years now," Reardon noted with pride. "I've been the only doctor here since nineteen-oh-four."

"So you probably know just about everybody in town."

The doctor chuckled. "If I don't know'em, they're not in this town. I've delivered pretty much every baby and treated everybody in this town for almost half a century."

"Then you know Susie Washburn," Kimble concluded.

Dr. Reardon froze for a moment, but recovered almost immediately, although not without Donnelly noticing. The doctor continued dressing Kimble's wound, but now his hands trembled slightly and he looked a little pale.

"Is that why you're here?" Reardon asked after a few moments. "To ask about Susie?"

"She was reported missing," chimed in Donnelly.

"Well, I wouldn't worry too much," the doctor stated. "She's probably just run off again."

"So her running away was common knowledge," Donnelly surmised.

Reardon shrugged. "I imagine so. I can't recall anyone mentioning it was a secret."

"What about her accidents?" Kimble inquired.

Dr. Reardon, finishing with the bandage, looked startled.

"I don't think I know what you mean," he declared. "By the way, you're good to go now."

Kimble got off operating table. His pants lay across the back of a nearby chair. He grabbed them and, grimacing, began putting them on while talking.

"Well," Kimble droned, "you're the person who would have treated Susie for any injuries, right?"

"Most likely," Reardon agreed.

"So would you say that her accidents were common knowledge – like her running away?"

"I'd say so," Reardon admitted. "It's not all that easy to hide an arm or a leg in a cast, you know."

Donnelly, hastily writing down the doctor's words, looked up. "So she had a history of having accidents?"

"No, no," the doctor stressed. "Only in the past few years."

Now dressed, Kimble frowned. "Didn't that strike you as unusual, that a young girl should suddenly start having so many accidents? Didn't it suggest something to you?"

"C-C-Can't say that it did, no," Reardon stammered, plainly nervous now.

Suddenly Kimble grabbed him near the neck of his lab coat and pulled him close. Donnelly, shocked, stopped writing and stared.

"Cut the shit, Doc!" Kimble yelled. "This girl was being beat, and you never reported it! Why?"

"Please! Please!" the doctor pleaded. "You're hurting me!"

Donnelly rushed over and attempted to pull his partner's hands off Reardon.

"Let him go!" Donnelly insisted. "Dammit, Billy! Get your hands off him!"

Kimble released his hold, but still looking furious, tried to come back towards the doctor. Donnelly pushed him back. Meanwhile, Reardon massaged his throat gingerly as he flopped down in a chair. He looked at the two agents warily.

"Look," he began, "Susie's daddy is–"

"The sheriff," Donnelly interjected. "Yeah, we know all that. What else?"

"The Sheriff, he's a good man," Reardon insisted, "but Susie was doing things, terrible things, and Zeke – that's the Sheriff – Zeke was out of control trying to make her mind."

Donnelly's brow crinkled. "What kinds of things was she doing?

"Things no respectable young lady would," Reardon replied.

"I see," Donnelly muttered. "Well, thanks for your help. What do we owe you?"

"It's on the house," the doctor said, plainly eager for them to depart.

"That's kind of you," Donnelly noted. "If we need anything else, we know where to find you."

The two agents then left. As soon as the door closed behind them, Reardon let out a sigh of relief. He then got up and went quickly to a telephone that was nearby and began dialing. It was answered on the second ring.

"Hello, Zeke?" the doctor began. "We got problems..."

Chapter 9

Dr. Reardon's office was located in a two-story red brick building. Coming down the steps that led up to the office door, the agents headed to their car, which was parked directly in front of the building.

"I can't believe the way you lost it up there," Donnelly noted as he headed to the driver's side of the car.

Kimble, getting in on the passenger side, stated, "It's called a Mutt-and-Jeff act, kid. Also known as good cop" – Kimble pointed at his partner – "bad cop." He then indicated himself with his thumb.

"Oh," Donnelly muttered as he started the car and began driving.

"Relax, kid," Kimble advised. "It takes two people working together for a while to get a good Mutt-and-Jeff act together, but I have to admit, you did a good job back there."

"Thanks," Donnelly said. "So what do you make of what the doc said about Susie?"

Kimble shrugged. "About her running off? It's possible, I suppose. But doing things "no respectable young lady" would do? That suggest anything to you?"

"Sex…what else? Now I can understand her Dad's attempts to control her."

"Maybe..." Kimble droned, not sounding completely convinced.

"So what next?"

"Next, we find a hotel," Kimble said, noting that it was starting to get dark.

****

To the surprise of neither agent, there was only one hotel in town and it didn't take long to locate it. Ergo, not long after leaving Dr. Reardon's office, they found themselves carrying their luggage into what a sign outside proclaimed to be the Broussard Hotel.

Looking around, they noticed that the lobby was small and filled with antiquated furniture, but meticulously clean. Heading to the front desk, they noted that there was no one on duty. However, there was a bell sitting on the counter, which they rang. A few moments later, a plainly bitter woman in her sixties quickly came through a door behind the counter. Wiping her hands on an apron she was wearing, she coldly assessed the agents before speaking.

"Can I help you?" she finally asked.

"Sure," answered Kimble. "Are you Mrs. Broussard?"

"It's 'Miss,'" she practically snapped. "What do you want?"

"A million bucks, if you've got it," Kimble quipped. "Barring that, we'll take a room."

Ms. Broussard, conspicuously unamused, eyed him testily for a few seconds. "Rent is twenty dollars a week. In advance."

She then held out her hand, palm up. Kimble, giving his partner a look of exasperation, pulled out his wallet. A moment later, Ms. Broussard was holding two crisp ten-dollar bills.

Shoving the money into a pocket, she said, "Follow me," and then headed to a nearby set of stairs. The two agents followed, and minutes later found themselves being shown into their new quarters.

The room was small and sparsely furnished with two beds and a dresser with a mirror. There were also two windows, one by each bed. Kimble tossed his luggage onto one of the beds and, spinning in a circle, eyed the room critically.

"Be it ever so humble..." he said.

Ignoring him, Ms. Broussard turned to Donnelly. "Here's your key." She then placed the item in his hand. "Bathroom's down the hall. As to the house rules, I don't allow no smokin', no drinkin', no gamblin', no parties, and no women."

With that, she stalked out of the room and shut the door, without giving her latest guests a chance to comment or ask questions.

Kimble flopped down on the bed he'd selected. "You know, I can't for the life of me figure out why a sweet, pretty thing like that isn't married."

"Because," Donnelly said as he took a seat on his own bed, "like all black widows, she mates…then she kills."

Kimble snickered at that as Donnelly stretched out with his hands tucked behind his head. Leaning to the side, Kimble pulled aside the curtains and peeked out the window.

"Looking at Ms. Broussard," Kimble continued, "I think it's more likely they died during the mating."

Donnelly, eyes closed, laughed. Kimble, still looking out the window, saw the main street of the town – currently lit by streetlights – nearly deserted. However, he noticed a restaurant almost directly across from them with several people inside. He turned to his partner.

"Hey, kid," Kimble said. "What do you say we go get something to eat?"

Chapter 10

As they exited the hotel and began walking across the street, Donnelly protested his partner's insistence that they go grab a meal.

"If you're hungry that's fine," Donnelly told him, "but why do I have to come along?"

"Because, it's not about food, you twit," Kimble blurted out. "It's about getting some information. A town this small doesn't have secrets. By tomorrow morning everyone in this town is going to know why we're here, and we're going to have a snowball's chance in hell of finding out anything after that, so we have to get everything we can now, before this town slams the door on us like a priest to a whore."

By that time they were getting close to the restaurant. Donnelly noticed that the place had a large plate glass window, on which were painted the words "RILEY'S BAR AND GRILL." There was also a sign in the window which declared, "WHITES ONLY." At that point they had reached the door and quickly went inside.

The bar, like the town, was fairly small. Two tables, currently occupied by graying old men, sat in front of the window. Three booths ran flush with the back wall, and a number of stools were lined up in front of the bar.

A young Black man was patiently sweeping the floor. Behind the bar stood the owner, Riley – a middle-aged man with a five o'clock shadow and greasy, slick-backed hair. He was polishing a beer mug and had been watching uneasily as the two agents – in deep conversation – approached the bar and stepped inside.

All conversation came to a halt when Kimble and Donnelly entered, and all eyes turned to them. Donnelly looked around warily, but Kimble acted as if nothing had happened. He headed straight to the bar and his partner followed.

"Good evening," Kimble said to the man behind the counter.

"Howdy," Riley replied.

"What's on the menu?" inquired Kimble.

In response, Riley tapped a menu board hanging above him and stepped to the side, watching the two men closely. Kimble stared at the menu, seemingly in deep thought. The listed options appeared to be novel dishes, to say the least: FROG LEGS, GREENS, PIG FEET, GATOR…

Donnelly stared at the menu in shock and gulped audibly.

"Boy, oh boy," Kimble muttered. "So much to choose from. Truthfully though, I'm not really hungry. Trevor, you're the one who wanted something to eat; what would you like?"

Donnelly slowly turned to stare at Kimble, his face mingling a look of dread and anger, as well as disgust.

"Uh, I'm not as hungry as I thought," Donnelly finally said.

At this, Riley burst into laughter, and the others in the restaurant joined in. The two agents looked around in bewilderment, realizing that everyone was laughing at them. Riley shook his head sadly, and conversation in the bar resumed.

"Damn city slickers!" Riley uttered, still grinning. Turning to the agents, he said, "How about a coupla ham sandwiches?"

"Sounds fine," Kimble told him. "Just bring them over to the booth if you would."

"Sure," Riley said. Nodding towards the Black man sweeping the floor, he stated, "Luthor will bring them to you in a minute."

The two agents then headed for one of the empty booths near the back wall. They slid in facing each other.

Speaking in a low tone, Kimble said, "Alright, what do we know so far? Number one: Susie was a morally loose girl. Number two: her father tried to keep her in line any way he could. Number three: she tried repeatedly to run away from home. Sound right so far?"

"Yeah," Donnelly agreed. "Then she disappeared, and no one in this town cared to report her missing."

"Not everyone," his partner countered. "Don't forget Ginger Meadows."

Donnelly grunted noncommittally as Luthor approached with two sandwiches on plates. A young man in his mid-twenties, he gingerly set the plates down while keeping his head lowered.

"Dollar fifty," Luthor mumbled softly.

Kimble pulled out his wallet and placed two dollars on the table. He then took out a third dollar and held it between his thumb and forefinger, making sure Luthor saw it, but keeping it hidden from anyone else in the bar other than his partner.

"My friend and I are having a little problem," Kimble stated, "and we were wondering if you could help us out."

As he spoke, Kimble carefully folded the dollar bill and tucked it under his plate. Luthor merely watched without comment.

"See," Kimble went on, "we're trying to get some information and we've been running into some trouble. If you can help us, we can make it worth your–"

He was interrupted by Riley's voice, cutting through the air like a knife, saying, "Luthor! What are lolly-gagging over there for? Get your nigger-ass outside and sweep off the sidewalk, and then take out the trash. I ain't paying you to stand around and breathe!"

Luthor quickly spun around towards Riley and answered in a subservient tone. "Yessir." Turning back to Kimble, he asked, "Take your plate, sir?"

"Yes, please," Kimble replied as he grabbed his sandwich off the dish. "I don't really need it."

Luthor bent over the table and carefully lifted up the plate with the dollar under it. He then whispered under his breath. "Outside. Ten minutes."

Kimble nodded almost imperceptibly as Luthor shuffled back towards the kitchen.

Chapter 11

Donnelly found himself a little stunned by what had happened between Kimble and Luthor, and was almost awed by the swiftness of the exchange between them. Following his partner's lead, he began eating his sandwich, but after a moment decided to speak up.

"What was that all about?" he asked.

"It was about getting information," Kimble explained.

"By bribing someone?"

"It's not a bribe," Kimble insisted. "A bribe is money or favors given to influence or corrupt. What I've done is offer an extra incentive for doing the right thing, like giving your kid a nickel for making an 'A' in school."

At that moment, Luthor – broom in hand – came out of the kitchen and walked towards the front door.

"Luthor!" Riley shouted all of a sudden.

Luthor stopped dead in his tracks. Riley, absolutely furious, swiftly came from behind the bar and approached him.

"What the hell do you think you're doing?" Riley demanded.

Luthor licked his lips nervously. "G-g-going to sw-sw-sweep the side–"

His words were cut off as Riley struck him on the ear with a blow that sent Luthor sprawling. Donnelly started to rise but Kimble grabbed his arm and shook his head, indicating that he shouldn't interfere.

Riley stood over Luthor, yelling. "You know better than that, dammit! You come in and go out through the back!"

Rising shakily, Luthor simply nodded. "Yessir." Eyes lowered, he headed to the kitchen.

Obviously still angry, Riley suddenly noticed Kimble and Donnelly staring at him.

"Sorry about that, gents," he apologized, "but these damn jungle bunnies are really starting to get uppity. It's about all a man can do to keep'em in their place."

"It's alright," Kimble assured him. "The whole world's going crazy like that. Blacks getting uppity, Communism taking over, children listening to rock 'n roll instead of their parents."

"You hit the nail right on the head, mister," Riley remarked as he walked back behind the bar. "I've got a sixteen-year-old who won't listen to anything else. He's as hardheaded as they come."

Kimble simply nodded in understanding.

"Speaking of wayward kids," Donnelly chimed in, "do you happen to know a girl by the name of Susie Washburn?"

Riley simply stared at him, as did the other customers in the restaurant. Kimble wiped his face with his hand.

"Shit…" he muttered under his breath.

Donnelly suddenly flashed his badge for all to see.

"I'm Special Agent Donnelly," he announced, "and this is Special Agent Kimble. We're with the FBI. Does anyone here have knowledge of the whereabouts of Susie Washburn?"

No one spoke or moved for a moment. Then one of the old men rose and put his hat on his head, saying, "Well, it's getting late. See ya later, Riley."

He began walking towards the door, and his compatriots quickly followed his lead, making similar statements.

"Yeah, I'd better be getting back myself."

"Me, too."

"The wife'll sic the dogs on me if I'm not back soon."

In short, within roughly a minute, there was no one left in the place but the agents and Riley.

"Did you hear my question?" Donnelly asked Riley.

"Yeah, I heard you," Riley muttered contemptuously.

"Well?" Donnelly demanded. He glanced at his partner, but Kimble had returned to eating his sandwich and was merely watching the exchange between the other two men.

"Well what?" Riley shot back.

"Do you or don't you know Susie Washburn?" Donnelly queried.

"I don't know where she is, if that's what you mean," Riley told him.

"No, I'm asking if you know her."

Riley crossed his arms defiantly. "I think you boys need to be talking to Zeke, the sheriff."

"We'll get around to him, but right now we're talking to *you*."

"Well, right now, I've got nothing to say."

Kimble, finally taking a break from eating his sandwich, raised a finger. "If I may make a point?"

Looking at Donnelly for approval, he received it in the form of a curt nod, at which point he turned to Riley.

"You do realize that this is a federal investigation, don't you?" he asked. "And you realize that by refusing to cooperate we can bring charges against you?"

"Charges?" Riley echoed, looking perplexed. "For what?"

"Well, let's see…" Kimble intoned. "Impeding a federal investigation, obstruction of justice–"

"Conspiracy," added Donnelly.

"Malfeasance," continued Kimble.

Riley's eyes blinked rapidly and his mouth dropped open in awe and fear as the agents' list of offenses continued to grow.

"And there's judicious onslaught," Donnelly noted.

Kimble cocked an eyebrow at this, seeming to suggest that Donnelly was pushing the envelope, before rounding out the list himself with "Anal retentiveness."

Donnelly fought to keep from smiling at that last one. Riley, however, had seemingly had enough.

"Alright, alright!" Riley said, throwing up his hands in defeat. "I'll tell you what I know."

Chapter 12

The two agents sat patiently waiting for Riley to speak. On his part, Riley took a deep breath, and then started talking.

"I know her," he said. "I mean, I *knew* her. But Susie was a bad seed. Everybody knew it, and everybody admired the way Zeke tried to handle things."

"By beating her," Donnelly concluded.

"Maybe it sounds harsh to you," Riley stated, "but there's no other way to control kids. It's too bad it didn't work, 'cause she was a pretty little thing. Grew up to be the spitting image of her mother, and everybody loved that woman."

"So what happened to her?" Kimble asked.

"She died in a fire," Riley explained, "along with Zeke's brother who was there visiting."

"And now the daughter's missing," Donnelly pointed out.

"They say tragedies happen in threes," Riley offered, "although I don't think I'd call Susie missing a tragedy."

"Why?" inquired Kimble. "What else do you know?"

Riley, looking nervous, spent a moment wiping his forehead. He then let out a deep sigh and was on the cusp of saying something when the door opened and a young guy came in. He appeared to be in his mid-twenties and wore cowboy boots, a ten-gallon hat, and a western vest sporting a badge that said "Deputy."

"Hey, Riley," the newcomer said, walking straight up to the bar. "Zeke said to be on the lookout for two…"

He trailed off when he suddenly noticed that Riley wasn't looking at him. Following the man's gaze, the deputy finally took notice of Kimble and Donnelly sitting in the booth. Kimble smiled at him.

"Howdy," Kimble said in an affable tone.

The deputy gave Riley a judgmental glance before turning back to the two agents.

"Howdy yourself, stranger," he intoned, returning Kimble's smile. Taking a toothpick from the bar, he put it in his mouth and sauntered over to the booth.

"Deputy Sheriff William Conners at your service," he announced to the agents. "Mind if I take a seat?"

"Not at all," Donnelly told him. "I'm Special Agent Donnelly; this is Special Agent Kimble."

Kimble gave a nod at the introduction then went back to eating his sandwich while Conners pulled a chair up to the outside of their booth, turning it backwards before flopping down into it. Chewing on his toothpick, he spent a moment looking from Kimble to Donnelly, as if sizing them up in some way.

"Now as I understand it," Conners began, "you boys have been asking a few questions about Susie Washburn."

"That's right," Kimble confirmed.

"Not to step on anybody's toes, you understand, but around here a man's business is considered his own," Conners stated. "It's a private thing and should stay that way. You agree?"

"Yes," Kimble said, "but–"

"Now, now, now," Conners interjected. "No 'buts.' You agreed with me."

As he spoke, a large black beetle somehow found its way onto the table and began to waddle slowly across it.

Conners slowly drew a stately Bowie knife out of his boot, all the while watching the insect.

"Now, seeing as these things you're asking about are of a personal nature," Conners went on, "I'd advise you to quit while you're ahead. Everyone's got their place in the world, and stepping into someone else's spot just throws everything out of whack. Only trouble can come of dipping your bucket in another man's well. A fella could get hurt."

Quick as a flash, Conners struck with the knife, impaling the beetle on the tip of his blade, where it struggled in vain.

"A man who does that is like a bug scampering into the light," the deputy continued. "He's asking to get stepped on."

As he finished speaking, Conners placed the tip of his knife under the heel of his boot and pressed down, crushing the beetle as he drew the knife back.

He then looked from Kimble to Donnelly, before uttering, "Understand?"

"I think we do," Donnelly replied.

"Good," the deputy stated. "Then I'll tell the sheriff that you two will probably be on your way some time tomorrow. Nice to see how things worked out."

Conners got up to leave, but had barely taken two steps before Donnelly's voice brought him up short.

"But you do know that, sometimes, you can't just mind your own business," Donnelly noted. "Sometimes the world won't let you. Like around twelve years ago. This country tried to mind its own business, and the Japanese bombed us anyway. So we came into the war and kicked ass. It's what you have to do sometimes. Understand?"

The deputy's eyes narrowed for a second, then he smiled, saying, "I expect we'll be meeting again. Under other circumstances."

"I guess we will," Donnelly agreed.

Rather than respond, Conners merely tipped his hat, turned, and left the restaurant.

Once the deputy had departed, Kimble leaned over and clapped Donnelly on the shoulder.

"You did well, kid," Kimble declared. "Come on, let's get out of here."

The two of them then slid out of the booth. Riley watched silently as they walked to the exit and left. As soon as they were gone, he reached for a telephone located beneath the bar.

Chapter 13

Luthor was sweeping the sidewalk as the two agents left Riley's place. Stopping in front of him, Kimble inconspicuously crumbled up a dollar bill and dropped it onto the pile of trash Luthor was sweeping up.

"If anybody asks," Kimble explains, "you're giving us directions to the sheriff's office." Getting a nod from Luthor in return, he went on. "Now, what do you know about Susie Washburn?"

True to his part, Luthor turned and pointed a finger down the street to a sign in front of a local building that read "SHERIFF." At the same time, he started speaking.

"Not much, sir," he admitted. "She the sheriff's daughter, but she run off a coupla times – didn't come back last time. Then there was the thing with Jaspar."

As Luthor was talking, Kimble glanced around casually. He didn't see anyone on the street, but he did notice Riley through the plate glass window of his bar. The man was talking animatedly on the telephone, although he seemed to stiffen when he realized Kimble was looking at him.

"What do you mean 'the thing with Jaspar'?" asked Donnelly, bringing Kimble back to the conversation at hand. "Jaspar who?"

"Well, sir," Luthor replied, "she was–"

He abruptly stopped speaking when the bar door suddenly flew open and Riley began yelling at him.

"Dammit, Luthor!" Riley bellowed. "I give one of you tar-babies a chance, and you want to pussyfoot around like you're at a watermelon picnic! Finish sweeping that sidewalk and get in here – we're closing early tonight!"

"Yes, sir!" Luthor shouted back, then went back to sweeping.

Kimble, speaking loud enough for Riley to hear, said, "Thanks for the directions, Luthor. I knew the Sheriff's office was somewhere around here."

He and Donnelly then continued on their way.

****

Sheriff Ezekiel Washburn's house was a wooden, two-story structure located at the end of a dirt road. It was unassuming in appearance, and – having been built just thirty years earlier – was considered 'contemporary' by Evangeline standards. At present, the house was dark except for a light in the living room.

Typically peaceful and serene after sunset, the normal tranquility of the sheriff's homestead was disturbed by the presence of a police car that came barreling up the road to the house. Deputy Conners, behind the wheel, braked hard and came to a screeching halt directly behind the sheriff's parked car. Jumping out, he raced up the porch steps and rushed inside without bothering to knock.

The front door opened into the living room, which was currently empty. Two easy chairs and a sofa were arranged around a beat-up coffee table, on which sat two empty beer cans. There was also a radio in a nearby corner. The only other things of note were a pair of swinging doors that led to the kitchen, and a set of stairs that led up to the second floor.

"Zeke!" Conners called out. "Zeke!"

Looking around anxiously, the deputy was caught by surprise when Sheriff Wasburn entered the room, casually meandering through the swinging kitchen doors.

He was a big man, well over six feet in height and a bit overweight. Just entering middle age, a slowing metabolism had caused him to develop a prominent beer belly. However, this caused him little concern, as evidenced by the fact that he currently held a beer in one large, meaty hand. Pot belly notwithstanding, most folks found him intimidating because of his size, and he generally used it to full effect.

"Zeke," Conners began, "those two FBI guys–"

"I know, I know," Washburn drawled, cutting his deputy off. "I just got off the phone with Riley. Seems like they wasted no time talking to people."

As he finished speaking, the sheriff set his beer on the coffee table and wandered over to a closet next to the stairs.

"People?" Conners echoed as Washburn opened the closet and began fiddling around inside. "People like who? None of us will talk. Who could they learn anything from?"

"Take a guess," said the sheriff as he turned from the closet and tossed two cloth items onto the sofa: a Klan robe and hood.

Chapter 14

Kimble and Donnelly were getting ready for bed, each on his respective side of their hotel room.

Kimble glanced at his partner. "So what do you think of your first assignment so far, kid?"

Donnelly let out an exasperated sigh. "Look, let's get something straight: I'm not a kid. I'm a fully authorized agent of the FBI. That's number one. Number two, I'm your partner, and it decreases my effectiveness as an agent when you constantly call 'kid' in public. Number three–"

"Alright, kid – Trevor – you've made your point," Kimble conceded. "It's just an expression. No offense meant."

Donnelly grudgingly accepted the apology with a nod of his head. "None taken."

He then climbed into bed, taking a moment to get comfortable under the sheets. Following this, he reached for a lamp that was on a nightstand next to his bed and turned it off. On his side of the room, Kimble – also now in bed – did the same.

"By the way," Kimble intoned, "what the hell is this 'judicious onslaught' you threatened to charge Riley with? Doesn't sound like any crime I ever heard of."

Donnelly chuckled. "Damned if I know, but it sounds a lot more like a crime than 'anal retentiveness.'"

"No argument there," Kimble stated, snickering.

****

Inside Riley's bar, Riley was behind the counter cleaning out the cash register while Luthor wiped off the booths and tables. Coming from behind the counter, Riley took his coat from a nearby coat rack and put it on while speaking to Luthor.

"Alright," Riley said, "I'm trusting you to lock up tonight, and if you do a good job, I just might start leaving you here to do it every night…give you a little more responsibility and experience."

"Yes, sir," Luthor acknowledged with a nod. "Thank you. Much appreciated."

"See you in the morning," Riley told him.

Following this, Riley stepped outside and sauntered down to the sidewalk. Once there, he paused and looked down the street towards the sheriff's office, where a truck was parked. Riley nodded once at the truck. The truck's headlights flashed on and off two quick times. Riley looked back through the bar's window at Luthor, who was still wiping tables and hadn't noticed anything. Smiling to himself, Riley walked quickly around the corner to his own car, at which point he got in and drove away.

****

Back in their hotel room, Kimble and Donnelly both appeared to be sleeping. (In fact, Donnelly had dozed off within minutes of getting under the sheets.) With the lights still out, Kimble quietly got out of bed. Constantly glancing in the direction of his partner, he slipped into his clothes and departed. As soon as the door closed, Donnelly opened his eyes. Slowly, he sat up in bed and noticed that Kimble was gone. He frowned for a moment, then lay down again and went back to sleep.

****

Finally finished for the night, Luthor came out of the kitchen at Riley's and began turning off all the lights in the bar. After checking the front door, he then went through the kitchen and exited out the back, locking the door behind him. Leaning against the wall outside was a bicycle. Luthor got on it and began riding away from the bar.

Not far away, Sheriff Washburn and his deputy sat in the front of a pickup truck, wearing their Klan robes. In the back of the truck were six other men dressed similarly, all hunkered down to keep out of sight. Conners, sitting behind the wheel, watched as Luthor came pedaling from behind the bar-and-grill.

"There he goes," Conners observed. "Stupid nigger…"

Conners then started the truck, but kept the headlights off as Luthor rode across the street and disappeared down an alley between two buildings.

Leaning out the window, the sheriff yelled into the back of the truck, saying, "Alright boys, this is it!"

On cue, everyone pulled on their Klan hoods as the truck began coasting down the street, heading on a direct intercept course with Luthor.

Chapter 15

Luthor rode in a leisurely fashion down a dirt road that was part of his usual route home. There were no streetlights along this particular thoroughfare, but enough moonlight filtered through the trees for him to see where he was going.

Although eager to get to his house, he was too tired to put more effort into pedaling. As usual, Riley had worked him to the bone. Riley clearly wasn't the best boss Luthor had ever had, but he was far from the worst – despite his tendency to get rough on occasion. His actions earlier, when he had knocked Luthor down in the bar, were a prime example.

That said, in Luthor's opinion, getting struck had been entirely worth the two dollars he'd gotten from the two visitors in town. For extra money like that, he'd take getting hit every day.

Those thoughts and more flitted through Luthor's mind as he rode his bike. Right about then, however, he started to hear something – a noise that he recognized almost immediately: the sound of a vehicle approaching.

Given how often cars passed him as he rode his bike, it was a sound he was quite familiar with. From what he could tell, the vehicle was coming up on him from behind. In fact, less than a minute later, he got the feeling that it was right on his tail, but for some reason the driver didn't have his headlights on. That's when Luthor got an awful feeling in the pit of his stomach. Suddenly full of dread, he glanced over his shoulder.

As luck would have it, that was the exact moment when the driver, Conners, turned on the headlights of the truck he was in. The sudden brightness made Luthor squint, but he turned forward again and began pedaling as fast as he could. No longer trying to be stealthy, the Klansmen in the back of the truck – brandishing baseball bats, clubs, and other weapons – began taunting their quarry as they gained on him.

"Yo ass is mine, boy!"

"We gone teach you a lesson about talkin' too much, nigger!"

"Say yer prayers, Sambo!"

The Klansmen anxiously tapped their bats and weapons against the side of the truck, urging it to go faster. In moments they caught up, pulling up next to Luthor. Suddenly Conners swerved, running Luthor off the road.

Away from the thoroughfare, the ground dropped steeply, and Luthor found himself struggling to steer as the bike went racing down a sharp incline. He had almost managed to regain control when his front tire struck a tree stump and he went flying.

He landed awkwardly with an audible thud and continued sliding down until the ground leveled off. At that point, the truck had stopped and the Klansmen jumped out. Quickly scanning the area below with flashlights, they soon spied Luthor struggling to his feet.

"Get 'im!" shouted Conners, and a moment later his fellow Klansmen charged.

Shirt torn and in obvious pain, Luthor watched their approach for a few seconds before limping off through the dark to the shelter of some nearby trees. Looking back, he saw two of the Klansmen trip and go sliding down. Plainly terrified, Luthor continued moving.

Once at the bottom of the slope, the Klansmen regrouped then spread out. Luthor, injured and tired, knew he had little chance of outrunning them. That being the case, he decided to hide, huddling down in a large bush near the edge of the swamp. However, he had barely gotten in position before he heard someone approaching.

It was a Klansman, of course, decked out in a robe and hood. Luthor watched as the man stealthily approached his hiding spot.

"Nig-ger…" the Klansman intoned in a singsong voice. "Nig-ger… Come out, come out wherever you are."

The man stopped right next to the bush where Luthor was hiding and looked out over the swamp. A huge alligator floated in the water about twenty feet from shore.

After staring at the reptile for a few seconds, the Klansman muttered, "Wow, you are one big, ugly sumbitch."

Suddenly Luthor jumped up and gave the hooded figure a huge shove, sending him out into the water. The gator moved towards the man, who began screaming like a woman as he tried to get to shore. Luthor was already moving again by then, but – glancing back – he saw the man's hood come off as he struggled to get to solid ground. It was Deputy Conners.

Other Klansmen hurried to the deputy's aid. For a moment, Luthor felt relief as concern for their colleague seemed to have made them forget about him. Still he risked a glance over his shoulder to make sure he wasn't being followed. He then turned back around – just in time to be struck on the jaw by a bat held by Sheriff Washburn, who stepped quietly from behind a tree.

The sheriff was wearing his Klan robe, but didn't have his hood on at the moment. He looked down at Luthor, who lay on the ground, semi-conscious, with his head lolling from side to side.

"Boy," he said to Luthor, "you 'bout to have the worst day since the Good Lord let the devil has his way with Job."

Chapter 16

Kimble was still asleep when Donnelly walked into their room with coffee and a bag of donuts the next morning. Apparently not enthused about finding his partner still in bed, Donnelly intentionally slammed the door as he came in.

Startled awake, Kimble suddenly sat up muttering, "Who? What..?"

Donnelly walked over and put a cup of coffee in his hand, saying, "Top o' the morning to ya."

Kimble rubbed the sleep out of his eyes with his free hand and sipped his coffee with the other. He then reached for his watch from the nightstand as Donnelly went to his own bed and sat down.

"Seven-thirty!" Kimble blurted out.

Donnelly nodded. "Yeah, I thought it wouldn't hurt to let you sleep late while I went out for coffee and donuts."

"Late? Geez, Trevor, the Almighty doesn't get up this early."

"That's because the Good Lord, being all-powerful and all-knowing – omniscient and omnipotent – can add a few extra hours to the day if HE finds himself short on time. We can't."

Rather than respond, Kimble merely groaned. Reaching out, he took the bag that Donnelly was holding and retrieved a donut from it. He bit into it, then nodded in satisfaction.

"Not bad," he acknowledged. "Where'd you get these?"

"From a little bakery right down the street," Donnelly replied.

"In a town this size, everything is right down the street. But since you seem to be in charge here today, dictating when we rise and shine, what do you think our plan should be?"

"Well, I think it's time we followed up on the lead Merrill Wright gave us: Ginger Meadows. We'll see what she has to say and go from there."

Kimble shook his head. "Negative."

"So what's wrong with that plan?" Donnelly inquired with a frown. "She's all we've got right now, and proper procedure is that we question her as soon as possible."

"Don't you remember what else Wright said? This woman took a chance getting the word out about Susie Washburn. You saw how close-lipped everybody is on this subject – the Doc, Riley, everybody at the bar. If we go straight to this woman and she does give us something we can use, we're pointing the finger directly at her as the stool pigeon."

Donnelly reflected on that for a moment, then asked, "So what do we do?"

"We talk to her, but only after we talk to a bunch of other people. Then, we talk to even more people afterwards."

"And if this 'bunch of other people' doesn't have anything we can go on?"

Kimble let out an exasperated sigh. "We don't give a rat's ass if they do or don't! All we're trying to do is protect this woman – this Ginger Meadows. No one in this horseshit town has the authority to make us divulge our sources, so if they ask anything in that regard, we tell them to shove it up their ass. But if we only talk to Ginger Meadows, they don't have to ask, and she ends up with her tits in some gator's belly. Therefore, we talk to a lot of people and generate confusion as to the source of our information."

"Oh," Donnelly muttered softly.

"You're damn right, 'Oh,'" his partner grumbled.

Donnelly didn't respond to this; he just sat on the bed, eyes downcast. Seeing this, Kimble sighed and ran his fingers through his hair.

"Look, kid – I mean, Trevor," he continued. "I didn't mean to come down hard on you, but–"

"No, no," Donnelly interjected. "You're right…I wasn't thinking. Guess you made your point."

"About what?"

"About some things being bullshit."

"Well, like I said before," Kimble explained, "it's not so much bullshit as it is recognizing what's really just a guideline and what isn't. But don't feel bad; this isn't the kind of thing they teach at the academy. You're doing fine, so don't be too hard on yourself. Now, give me fifteen minutes to shower and shave, and we can get rolling."

Chapter 17

Kimble drove as the two agents headed down a country road. Their destination was a mid-sized, two-story building – the local school. En route, Donnelly noticed small cabins made of rotting wood dotting both sides of the road.

"What are those?" he asked. "Some kind of storage sheds?"

Kimble shook his head. "Abandoned houses."

"People actually lived in those?"

"Yep."

Donnelly ruminated on that as they continued on their way. Minutes later, they arrived at the school.

"Any particular reason why we're coming here first?" Donnelly quizzed as his partner parked the car.

"Well, we know that Susie was having sex, right?" Kimble replied. "So who do young, teenage girls have sex with?"

"Young teenage boys," Donnelly answered.

"Exactly," his partner intoned as they got out of the car.

"You think that it was a boy from this school?"

"Well," Kimble said, "considering that it's the only school in town, I'd say it's a safe bet."

With that, the two men headed inside, and a short time later found themselves in the office of the school principal, Mr. Palmer. He was a slight, bespectacled man with a no-nonsense attitude. After learning that the agents were there in regard to Susie Washburn, he leaned back in his chair behind his desk, eyeing them critically.

"I'm not sure what I can do for you," he said after a few seconds. "Don't get me wrong, I definitely want to help, but I can't really offer a lot of information."

"Can't?" Donnelly inquired. "Or won't?"

"Can't," insisted Palmer. "See, I don't know enough about Susie to say anything relevant."

"And why is that?" Kimble asked. "A town this size, you're bound to know everything about everybody."

"Sure, but not in the way you think," Palmer stated. "Oh, I can tell you who she is, where her parents work, what her grandfather did that made him a legend in this town, and so on. What I can't do, though, is tell you about Susie the *person*, because I don't know her."

Donnelly looked at him skeptically. "So, there's nothing you can tell us?"

"'Fraid not," Palmer replied.

"What about her school records?" Donnelly asked.

"Huh?" Palmer muttered in confusion.

"Maybe there's something in her record that could help us," Donnelly explained.

Palmer shook his head. "I don't think so."

"Maybe you should let us decide that," suggested Kimble.

"I'm not sure if I can," Palmer remarked. "School records are private and–"

"Maybe you don't understand, Mr. Palmer, but this is a federal investigation," Kimble reminded him. "If I feel that you're not fully cooperating, I can bring charges against you – starting with obstruction of justice."

"Impeding a federal investigation," Donnelly chimed in.

"Conspiracy," noted his partner.

"Judicial onslaught..." added Donnelly.

"Judicial onslaught?" Palmer unexpectedly uttered in confusion. "What the hell is that?"

The agents were silent for a moment, then Kimble bellowed, "Nevermind what it is! If you want a definition, I can show you better than I can tell you! Now, are you going to give us that file or not, 'cause right now there's nothing I'd like more than runnin' one of you rednecks in and working you over until I get to the bottom of this thing!"

Palmer, looking angry, reluctantly opened a drawer on his desk and pulled out a file folder. He slid it across his desk towards the agents. Donnelly picked it up and opened it.

"That there's her school record," Palmer explained. The two agents exchanged a glance, their looks conveying that both thought it odd how Palmer had Susie's file at-the-ready.

"Up until about two years ago, all A's and B's," Palmer continued. "A model student in just about every way, so I never saw her except in passing. Me, I only deal with the bad seeds – the misfits who think school is just a place for them to practice the disobedience they perfect at home. Even when her grades slipped, Susie was never one of those."

"Hmmm," Kimble mused. "We've been given the impression she was."

"Not on my watch," Palmer told them. "My only concern was how she acted in here; outside these four walls, what she did was her daddy's concern."

"And she was a student here all her life?" queried Donnelly.

"Yep," Palmer noted with pride. "We cover all grades here: kindergarten through twelfth."

"Then she must have had friends here," Kimble surmised. "Maybe even a boyfriend."

"It's possible…" Palmer noted somewhat nervously.

"Maybe we could talk to them," Kimble said. "Do you have a private room anywhere around here?"

"No, I'm afraid I don't," Palmer declared. "And with that…" He glanced at his watch as he trailed off, at the same time coming to his feet. "…I'm afraid I'll have to cut this short. I just remembered I have an appointment."

The two agents rose out of their seats. Palmer, coming from behind his desk, extended his hand, which Kimble and Donnelly shook in turn.

"Thanks for your time," Kimble told him. "We really appreciate it."

"No problem at all," Palmer insisted as he retrieved Susie's file and put it back in his desk. "Glad to do it."

At that juncture, Donnelly – standing behind Kimble – started walking towards the exit but stopped when he saw that his partner hadn't moved.

Palmer and Kimble stared at each other. Palmer then looked at his watch again.

"Well," Palmer droned, "I really have to get going, so..."

"Oh, I'm sorry," Kimble apologized. "Please, don't let us keep you."

Kimble then turned away from Palmer and took off his jacket, which he tossed over the back of Palmer's chair before sitting in it. Next, he opened the drawer and pulled out Susie's file.

Palmer just stared at him for a moment, then exploded. "What do you think you're doing?!"

"Commandeering your office," Kimble answered. "We have to have a private place to talk to people, and since no other rooms are available, we'll take this one."

Donnelly, picking up on his partner's line of thinking, took off his own coat and had a seat as well.

"You can't do that," Palmer complained.

"Actually, I've already done it," Kimble retorted. "Now, was there anything else?"

"But...but..." Palmer stammered, clearly flustered.

"No 'but's,' dammit!" Kimble noted angrily, standing up. "We ask for your help and you feed us a load of bull, and then try to shuffle us out the door faster than shit through a goose! Well, no more Mr. Nice Guy!"

With that, he sat back down and began to look through the file. He ignored Palmer, who continued to stand, simmering.

Finally, Kimble glanced up at him. "Don't you have an appointment to get to?"

Fists clenched, Palmer left the office, slamming the door behind him. Donnelly watched him leave, then turned to Kimble, who was laughing.

"That the way you normally solicit cooperation?" Donnelly asked.

"No," Kimble admitted, "but when it's assholes like that, I wish it was." Laying the file aside, he said, "Come on, let's start talking to some of these people."

"Who?" Donnelly asked. "We've got no idea who Susie Washburn's friends were."

"We'll start with teachers and classmates," Kimble replied. "They'll have an idea of who she was friends with."

Donnelly nodded in agreement as Kimble turned and pulled a thin yearbook off a shelf behind him and began flipping through it.

"Sounds good to me," Donnelly stated. "But if they're like everyone else in this town, how do we get them to help us?"

"Let's just play it by ear," Kimble suggested.

Chapter 18

Over the next few hours, the agents interviewed a variety of teachers and students about Susie Washburn. Although everyone probably knew why they were there, each conversation generally started the same, with Kimble and Donnelly explaining that they were investigating a missing person case. This was typically followed by one of the agents asking, "What can you tell us about Susie?"

The responses they received from everyone were essentially uniform in terms of tenor and sentiment, starting positive but eventually giving way to a negative slant:

"She was a nice girl...very bright."

"Pretty smart. She always got A's and B's."

"Funny, and a lot of fun to be around."

"At least she used to be. Then she changed."

"She stopped coming to class…started hanging out with the wrong sort of people."

"The sheriff, he tried to keep her in line, but it didn't do no good."

"She was dead set on doing her own thang, and willing to run away to do it."

At that point in each interview, the agents typically only had one follow-up question, which was, "When you say 'the wrong sort of people', you mean her boyfriend?"

As before, the responses that they received from everyone mirrored each other – so closely, in fact, that one would almost have thought they had practiced:

"No, not Michael. He wasn't like that."

"Michael was a good kid."

"A great guy…"

"He really liked Susie, and the sheriff approved of them courting."

"It was the other one – Jaspar Johnson."

"Jaspar's the one she should have left alone."

"Michael, though, was really good for her."

"Everybody likes Michael."

"She really should have stayed with Michael…"

Several hours after they began, despite the respondents being fairly cooperative, the agents decided to bring the interviews to a halt. They hadn't spoken to everyone – not by a longshot – but with all the interviewees basically parroting the same information, more sit-downs seemed unlikely to pay huge dividends.

"I don't think there's much more to be gotten from most of the remaining teachers and students," Kimble stated. "And I'd rather not spend a bunch of time just spinning our wheels if we don't have to."

"Agreed," his partner said. "But if we want to be thorough, we should still talk to the rest of them – even if we don't learn anything new."

"We can always pick up where we left off if we need to chat with somebody," Kimble remarked. "But right now, there's probably only one of them that's worth talking to: the boyfriend – Michael."

"What about this Jaspar guy?" asked Donnelly.

"He's not in the yearbook," Kimble stated. "I looked for him the first time someone mentioned his name, and he's not in there."

Donnelly reflected on that for a moment. "So what are you thinking – older guy?"

"Or a dropout, which would fit with the overview that he was no good for Susie."

"Makes sense," Donnelly noted after pondering for a second. "But the boyfriend can probably confirm."

Kimble nodded, saying, "Let's get him in here."

****

Michael turned out to be a tall, handsome young man of seventeen. However, good looks and a well-toned physique had resulted in an arrogant demeanor and a sense of entitlement. At present, he sat in a chair facing the two agents across the principal's desk, arms crossed while he glared at Kimble and Donnelly.

"Can we get on with it?" Michael demanded, as if he were in charge.

"Easy, kid," said Kimble. "We just want to ask you–"

"I already know what you want to ask," Michael interjected. "The answer is yeah, I knew the slut. We were dating – kind of serious – then she left me for that...that...that damned nigger!"

The two agents shared a glance, then Donnelly asked, "You mean Jaspar?"

"Yes, dammit," Michael hissed. "Who the hell do you think I mean?"

"So, Jaspar's Black?" inquired Kimble.

"Of course he's Black!" Michael shot back angrily. "You think I'd be this pissed if she'd just fallen for another White guy? That slut! Do you know how embarrassing it was for me to have my girl leave me for a spear-chunker? Do you know what I had to put up with? Snickers and giggles behind my back all day long; nasty poems taped to my locker; little sketches of me picking cotton in a field while she and her nigger boyfriend sit on the porch drinking lemonade! That bitch! I hope they never find her. And if they do–"

Michael abruptly stopped speaking, apparently realizing he was on the verge of saying something that might not cast him in the best light.

"Go on," Kimble urged him. "If they do find her, then what?"

Michael leaned back in the chair, arms still crossed, and looked out the window.

"Nothing," he said in response to Kimble's question.

"Well, if they do bring her back," said Donnelly, "do you think she'll try to be with Jaspar again?"

Michael snorted in derision then smiled slyly. "Even if they do bring her back, that won't happen. That nigger's been fixed for good."

"What do you mean?" asked Donnelly.

Michael merely gave him a hard stare and declared, "That's all I have to say."

Chapter 19

Following their conversation with Michael, Kimble and Donnelly called the interviews to a halt. They then surrendered control of the principal's office back to Palmer, who glowered at them until they left the building.

"Nice kid, huh?" Kimble noted sarcastically as they got into their car.

"Who, Michael?" his partner responded. "Oh yeah, great guy…probably already a member of the Junior Klan League."

"So what do you think so far?" Kimble asked as he began driving back to town.

Donnelly pulled his notepad out and began reviewing it.

"Well, this Jaspar character obviously figures pretty highly," he said. "He was mentioned just about every time we brought Susie's name up. But at least we know now why he wasn't in the yearbook: the school's segregated. Still, he seems like somebody we should talk to."

"Same thing I was thinking," Kimble stated, "but I get the feeling we're gonna have to talk pretty loud for him to hear us."

Donnelly frowned. "Why do you say that?"

"Because he's probably dead."

"Huh?" Donnelly muttered incredulously.

"Small town like this," Kimble explained, "they're not gonna brook a Black man laying with a White woman. Couple that with what that kid back at the school just said, I bet you dollars to donuts that this Jaspar is six feet under."

"So, do you think they killed Susie, too?"

Kimble shrugged. "Hard to say…these things are always a little ornery."

"Sounds like you've experienced this kind of thing before."

"Well, I grew up in a small southern town something like this," Kimble stated. "Whites and Blacks separated and hating each other."

"What made you different?" inquired Donnelly.

"I wasn't. Just like young Mike back there, I was Junior Klan. I hated Blacks – the way they looked, the way they talked, the food they ate… But it wasn't just me; that was the attitude of the whole town. When I look back on it, I can't believe some of the things I would do back then. How I did everything in my power to make an entire race of people miserable just because they weren't the same color as me."

"What changed you?"

"The war," Kimble uttered flatly. "You're probably not old enough to remember much about it, but World War II had to be the single most significant event in the history of the planet. I mean, the whole world was at war, billions of people trying to get at each other's throats. And there I was, a young soldier – green as I could be – hoping to get in on the action."

Kimble chuckled in fond remembrance for a moment, then went on. "I was part of the Army's Light Infantry Division, forward based, and I loved it."

"You weren't worried about getting shot or killed?"

"Hell no! We were young and gonna live forever, so going to the front line was nothing to us. We weren't gonna die! Dying's what happened to some poor asshole in the next unit, not *us*! We were single-handedly gonna cut through the German lines, kick Hitler's ass, and then come home with a chest full of medals."

Kimble paused for a moment to collect his thoughts. When he started speaking again, his partner was listening intently.

"The night before we were being sent to the front lines," he said, "they gave us a party – a big send-off at a nightclub to get our spirits up. Basically a condemned man's final request, but we didn't know that then. Anyway, the party's in full swing when a group of Blacks come in."

"Now, this was over in Europe," he continued, "where they're a lot more tolerant of race than we are, and Blacks and Whites were allowed to mix in clubs, so no one noticed anything at first. Then one of our boys saw them. Within five minutes, all hell broke loose, and we'd come up with a new answer to the old question, 'What's black and white and red all over?'"

Kimble chuckled to himself, while Donnelly listened with rapt attention.

"We demolished that place," he said. "There wasn't a single table left standing when we got through. And I was right in the thick of it. I called one of them a nigger and hit him across the back with a chair. I smacked another across the temple with a bottle of gin. But I have to give those boys credit: they gave as good as they got. There wasn't a single guy who was there with me who wasn't black-and-blue the next day, which is also when we headed out to the front lines. That's when everything changed."

Kimble paused for a moment, then went on. "We weren't there three days before the Krauts had us running back with our tails between our legs. They pushed us back, hard and fast, and guys were dropping like flies along the way. Their planes took out everything we had, from aircraft to tanks to staff cars. We were on foot, literally running for our lives, all the excitement of war gone. And that's when it happened."

Kimble stopped for a second, prompting Donnelly to ask, "What? What was it that happened?"

"I took one in the back," Kimble told him. "Near the spine. Paralyzed my legs…I couldn't even feel them. And all I could think was that I was gonna die, so I just lay there screaming for help and begging for anyone to come get me, not to leave me. And then a voice came out of nowhere – another soldier. 'It's okay,' he said. 'I gotcha.' It was one of the Black guys from the bar…the one I had hit with the gin bottle."

"Did he recognize you?" quizzed Donnelly.

"Without a doubt," Kimble replied with a nod. "I saw the way his eyes lit up; he knew who I was, and he still had a nasty scar where the bottle broke and cut him. That's when I passed out, but apparently he picked me up, slung me across his shoulders, and started running. See, I didn't know it at the time, but those boys were our back-up. Nobody had ever meant to actually use them, but the Germans had cut us up so bad that they had to. So he ran with me back to a hospital, where they dug the bullet out and sent me home. It was a year before I could walk again, but during that time I found out just how far he carried me on his back."

Donnelly didn't try to mask his curiosity. "How far?"

"Five miles," Kimble declared, with admiration in his tone. "Five long-ass miles that big, Black sonuvabitch carried me, and I never even knew his name. I'd only met him once and that one time I tried to kill him, but he was willing to risk his life to save mine. Why? If the situation had been reversed, I would have left him; thank GOD it wasn't, though, because I learned a lot from that."

"Like what?"

Kimble pondered momentarily before answering. "You know, lying on your back in a hospital bed gives you a lot of time to think. There I was, supposedly the Great White Man, superior in all ways to every other race. And yet when it came down to it, one of those inferior people had done something that would never have occurred to me – performed a more noble act than I was ever capable of. So I had to ask myself, who was the better person, who was right and who was wrong, and how much of what I'd been taught was a lie."

"Must not have been easy," his partner surmised.

"It wasn't," Kimble admitted. "It's kinda hard to accept that everything you've been taught your whole life has been fabricated. It's a little like having your parents lie to you every year and tell you that there really is a Santa Claus, then catching your Dad putting all the presents under the tree. You suddenly know the truth, but it's not really possible to fully accept – at least not right away. Basically, it's been a long hard road, but I think I'm there now. I no longer hate Blacks and I don't support racist views. I simply live and let live."

At that point, he brought the car to a stop, and Donnelly noticed that they had arrived at Riley's Bar.

"Come on," said Kimble. "Let's grab some lunch."

Chapter 20

On this particular occasion, the bar was full of patrons when the agents went inside. As a result, it was louder and more boisterous than it had been during their initial visit. That said, there was a momentary hush when the agents entered, but conversation quickly resumed as Kimble and Donnelly went to the counter to place their order, thereby making it clear that they were merely there for a meal as opposed to official business.

Plainly noting the increased number of customers, Donnelly – speaking in a low tone to his partner – said, "Apparently this is a popular lunchtime spot."

"I'm guessing it's the *only* lunchtime spot," Kimble shot back.

Fortunately, despite the additional clientele, the two agents managed to get seated at a booth near the back after once again ordering sandwiches. However, it was immediately evident that the table had not been properly bussed, as it still contained bits and morsels from the last meal eaten there (which may have explained why the booth had been empty). Donnelly frowned in distaste at a number of crumbs and odd stains he noticed on the table.

"I guess having Luthor keep the tables clean is a little too much class for this place," he offered.

"Yeah," his partner concurred. "Any more class and the Ritz will find itself battling some mean competition."

Glancing around, both men noticed almost everyone watching them warily. However, the attention they received wasn't unexpected. They were essentially novelty items: curios that merited a look, but not much more than that. That said, having a bunch of eyeballs on them didn't bother Kimble and Donnelly, so they both simply chose to ignore it.

The only person who didn't seem to be watching them was Riley, who was running around trying to serve everyone – and doing an utterly poor job of it. The patrons were obviously upset.

"Hey Riley!" called out one of them. "Where's my gumbo?"

"I ordered greens with this," griped another.

"You forgot to give me a spoon!" whined a third.

It didn't take an expert to realize that Riley was clearly in over his head. Trying to be everywhere at once, he zipped by the booth at one point, tossing down a plate with two ham sandwiches onto the table in front of the agents. One of the sandwiches flopped off the plate and onto the half-clean table. Quick as a wink, both agents reached for the sandwich left on the plate. Donnelly grabbed it first, grinning broadly.

"Sorry, Charlie," he said to Kimble.

His partner shrugged and then, much to Donnelly's surprise, picked up the sandwich off the table. Brushing it lightly, he took a bite and looked around the diner. Riley was still running around helter-skelter, his arms full of plates.

"Geez, Riley!" someone called out. "I only get an hour for lunch! Can't you speed it up?"

"No, dammit!" Riley exclaimed. "I'm in here by myself today and this is the best I can do. If you don't like it, you can always go to somewhere else!"

Since there were few – if any – options (which Riley was well aware of), that seemed to halt most of the complaints. However, it did prompt someone to suddenly ask, "So where's Luthor?"

Riley didn't answer, but another patron said, "I'm afraid Luthor had a little accident last night..."

This was followed by a loud round of laughter in the diner from a large majority of the customers, like it was the best joke they'd heard in ages. Suddenly Donnelly stood up.

"What kind of accident?" he asked no one in particular.

His question was met with dead silence.

Chapter 21

Luthor was lying in bed asleep when the agents – accompanied by Luthor's wife, Hazel – entered his bedroom. His face had been beaten to a pulp. Both eyes were black and swollen shut, his lip was split, and his nose looked broken. In addition, his head was wrapped in gauze, as was his torso, and there was a cast on his left leg and right arm.

Kimble and Donnelly just stared at him in shock for a moment. After asking about it at Riley's Bar, they had – unsurprisingly – been unable to get any definitive information about Luthor's "accident." They had, however, been able to obtain directions to his house and had promptly departed after settling their tab.

Now that they were able to lay eyes on him, Donnelly had trouble keeping his emotions in check.

"Luthor!" he shouted. "Luthor, can you hear me? Who...who did this to you?"

Although it must have taken a Herculean effort, one of Luthor's eyes opened slightly and focused on Donnelly. In addition, he was able to move one arm feebly while issuing a low moan. Hazel, openly hostile to the agents, came next to him and put her hand on his head.

"He can't talk," she told them testily. "Doctor wired his jaw shut. Even if he could, it's talking to *you* that got him in trouble."

"So you're sticking to your story?" asked Kimble. "That he fell off his bike?"

Hazel glared at him for a moment. The fell-off-his-bicycle explanation was something she told them when they arrived asking about her husband. Obviously the agents weren't buying it, but Hazel stuck to her guns.

"Ain't that what I said happened?" she almost hissed.

Luthor moaned a little louder and reached for his wife. She took his hand, then bent down and gave him a kiss on his forehead.

"It's okay, baby," Hazel said to him. "I'm here."

"Maybe we should talk in the other room," Kimble suggested.

Hazel nodded, and all three left the bedroom, closing the door behind them. They were now in the living room of what the agents took to be a modest home. Two small boys, one about seven years old and the other maybe five, were playing with marbles on the floor. They both stopped and simply stared at the two White men with their mother.

"Bobby," Hazel said, "take yo lil' brother and go outside and play while I talk to these gentlemen."

The older boy, Bobby, nodded. "Okay, Momma."

Both boys went racing out the front door. Once they were gone, Hazel turned to the two agents.

"As I was saying," Kimble began, "we–"

"I think I've said everything I'm gonna," Hazel declared, cutting him off.

"Please," Donnelly implored. "We can help you with this. We can get the men responsible and bring charges against them."

"Look," Hazel argued, "it's hard enough with both of us working to try to keep a roof over our heads and food on the table, now I gotta make do all by myself. Who gonna take care of my boys if both me *and* my husband are all broke up, bodywise?"

She then pointed at Donnelly. "Are you?" Without waiting for an answer, she looked at Kimble. "You?"

Neither agent responded.

Hazel stared at them with contempt. "That's what I thought."

She then walked to the front door and opened it, plainly dismissing them. Heads down, the two agents headed to the door and stepped outside onto the porch.

Luthor and Hazel's house was located in an older but well-maintained neighborhood of equally cozy homes. As Kimble and Donnelly walked out, they were shocked to see the porch surrounded by Black people. It was as if the entire neighborhood was standing there. No one said anything; they simply stared at the two men. Hazel was about to close the door on them, but before she could, Donnelly turned to her.

"You have to understand," he began. "We didn't mean for this to happen. We didn't know."

"Ain't that always the case?" Hazel demanded. "White folks *never* know. But that's because you don't care. You don't care enough to *want* to know, unless it's about something you want."

"Look, all we want to do is help," Donnelly insisted. "But unless you work with us, there's nothing we can do. Unless you tell us something, our hands are tied."

Scowling, Hazel merely stood in the doorway without comment. Donnelly suddenly spun towards those who had gathered.

"And that goes for the rest of you, too!" he blurted out. "We can do something about what happened to Luthor, but you've got to help us."

He moved towards the crowd, but as he stepped off the porch they backed away from him, almost in unison.

"There's got to be one of you who's willing to take a chance and trust us. There's no need to be afraid. We can protect you. Talk to us. *Please.*"

The crowd continued backing away, keeping distance between themselves and Donnelly, like he was diseased in some way. Suddenly, Kimble placed his hand on Donnelly's shoulder.

"I think we can leave," Kimble stated. "We're not going to get anything else here."

Chapter 22

Donnelly had a look of forlorn detachment on his face as he and Kimble drove down a dirt road. Kimble gave him a sympathetic look.

"Look, Trevor," Kimble said, "you shouldn't take it so hard."

"I know," Donnelly agreed, "but how can we be expected to do our jobs if people won't cooperate with us?"

"You've got to look at it from their point of view," his partner suggested. "Whether we solve this case or not, you and I are only here for a short time. On the other hand, these people are probably going to be here for the rest of their lives. Maybe we can protect them while we're here, but once we're gone, things will go back to the way they were. We can't just expect them to allow us to throw a monkey wrench into the works and screw everything up. They'd rather just keep the system they have than try a new one – pick the devil they know rather than one they don't."

Donnelly nodded in agreement as Kimble brought the car to a halt and parked outside a small one-room schoolhouse. The building was obviously old, and clearly in need of some maintenance.

"Well, here we are," Kimble announced.

"Where, exactly?" Donnelly asked as they got out of the car. "What are we going to find here?"

"Here is where we'll find Ginger Meadows," his partner stated, "who you were so eager to talk to this morning."

As the men approached the door of the school, they heard singing from within.

"You hear that?" Kimble inquired.

Donnelly nodded. "Yeah. Sounds like *Amazing Grace*."

At that point, having reached the door, they opened it and went inside. Upon entering, Kimble and Donnelly found themselves in a small vestibule. Nearby was a set of double doors, from which the singing was coming. Each of the doors had a small glass window.

Peeking through the windows, they saw a small classroom, full of Black children of all ages and one White woman – presumably Ginger Meadows. The children were all at the front of the classroom, facing the rear. Ginger had her back to the agents and was directing the children with an orchestra wand. Kimble openly admired her shape from behind as the two men entered the room. He then winked at Donnelly, who rolled his eyes in exasperation.

Ginger, noticing the attention of the children switching to something behind her, turned around. That's when the agents got their first look her and noted two things: she appeared to be in her early thirties, and she was breathtakingly beautiful.

Ginger gestured with the wand and the children stopped singing. She then approached the two men.

"Can I help you?" she asked when she drew near.

Kimble, seemingly dumbstruck by her appearance, merely stared at her.

Donnelly gave his partner a disparaging glance, then spoke. "Miss Meadows? I'm Special Agent Donnelly, this is Special Agent Kimble. We're with the FBI. We'd like to–"

"Wait just a minute, please," Ginger interrupted. Turning back to her students, she called out, "Hattie Mae!"

At the same time, she motioned towards a young girl who strode forward quickly. She appeared to be about sixteen and was very pretty. Ginger gave her the wand.

"Hattie, I need to talk to these gentlemen," Ginger told her, "so I need you to finish up the next few songs for me."

"Okay, Miss Meadows," Hattie Mae replied. She then went back to where the other children were waiting and took over directing. As the singing began again, Ginger and the two agents stepped out into the vestibule where they couldn't be heard.

Ginger spent a few seconds appraising them, then said, "So, you two are here to stir up this hornet's nest."

Kimble smiled. "I guess it's no secret why we're here, then."

"Secret?" she echoed mockingly. "Who kidnapped the Lindbergh baby – now *that's* a secret. Whatever happened to Amelia Earhart – *that's* a secret. Why you're here – that is most definitely *not* a secret."

"Fair enough," noted Donnelly. "So what can you tell us about Susie Washburn?"

"Nice girl," Ginger replied. "Very smart. She was definitely going places in the world."

"How well would you say you knew her?" queried Kimble.

"I'd like to say very well, but I'm not sure," Ginger admitted. "Susie kept a lot inside – didn't really talk a lot about herself – but it was easy to see she was unhappy. About what, I didn't know at first, but I never pressed the issue, and it didn't seem to interfere with her work."

"Her work?" Kimble repeated inquisitively.

"Not 'work,' exactly," Ginger explained. "It wasn't anything she was paid for, but she volunteered here, helping me out with things around this place in her spare time. That's probably part of what got her in trouble."

Kimble frowned. "How do you mean?"

Ginger sighed. "This town has a lot of antiquated ideas about people and status...things are pretty much laid out in black and white, if you know what I mean. What I'm doing here – teaching Negroes to read and write – has made me something less than popular. Susie volunteering didn't do anything for her social life, either. She mostly just helped me grade assignments and tutor some of our hard-to-reach students, but that was enough."

"Enough for what?" asked Donnelly.

"For her father to beat her," Ginger declared matter-of-factly. "He's Klan, you know, and having a daughter working to help Negroes didn't do anything for his prestige. And her relationship with Jaspar didn't help either."

"That would be Jaspar Johnson," Kimble added for clarity.

"Yes," Ginger confirmed with a nod.

"We've been hearing his name a lot," Donnelly noted. "What exactly was his relationship with Susie?"

"He worked as a handyman at the sheriff's house," Ginger replied. "He started there about a year ago. From what I could tell, he and Susie got to be real good friends. Too good, I guess."

The two agents exchanged a knowing glance.

"So," Donnelly droned, "they were…?" As he trailed off, he made a vague gesture with his hands.

"That's the rumor," Ginger told them, "but nobody knows for sure. Susie never said, and I never asked. If being with Jaspar made her happy, who was I to tell her anything different?"

"What happened to him?" asked Kimble.

Ginger seemed to ponder for a moment. "He and Susie disappeared around the same time – about seven months ago. That's when I knew."

Donnelly raised an eyebrow. "Knew what?"

"That I'd never see them alive again," Ginger stated in a melancholy tone. "I just kept hoping that they'd get away from here, make it to some place where color didn't matter. But then they found him hanging from a tree. He had been...*mutilated*."

As she spoke that last word, she glanced down momentarily at a spot just below Donnelly's waist. He gulped and involuntarily covered his groin.

"And Susie?" Kimble asked.

"She was never found," Ginger answered. "And if he did that to Jaspar, I hate to think about what he probably did to her."

Kimble's brow creased in thought. "Who, the sheriff?" Ginger simply nodded, prompting him to add, "Do you have any proof of that?"

She threw up her hands in exasperation. "Who needs proof? The whole town knows it! Just ask anybody!"

"That's part of the problem," Donnelly explained. "See, nobody's willing to talk to us."

"Well, what did you expect?" Ginger demanded. "This is a close-knit community – the Whites are going to close ranks to protect their own, and the Negroes are going to keep silent for fear of ending up like Jaspar or Luthor."

"Why do you think they left Jaspar hanging from that tree?" she continued snappishly. "If they wanted to hide their dirty work, they would have dumped him in the swamp and let the gators have him. But they *wanted* him to be found...to serve as an example of what happens to niggers who touch a White woman! And Luthor is an example of what happens to niggers who talk!"

"Well, you can't just expect us to waltz in here and figure everything out on our own!" Donnelly admonished. "If these people aren't going to help us, then we should just pack our bags and leave!"

"Alright, that's enough you two!" Kimble uttered before Ginger could respond. "Now let's all just take a moment and calm down."

Ginger and Donnelly simply looked at each other, both still angry.

Finally, Donnelly let out a pent-up breath. "Okay, Miss Meadows – is it okay if I call you Ginger?"

"No," she stressed heatedly, crossing her arms.

"Miss Meadows, then," Donnelly said. "I apologize. I'm a bit of a hot-head, I'm afraid, and I don't always watch my temper the way I should."

She eyed him for a moment, then seemed to relax. "It's okay. I'm just all wound up about this thing. I guess I just haven't thought about how hard it is for you to do your job without any help."

"Isn't there anyone we could possibly talk to?" Kimble asked.

Before she could respond, the doors to the classroom suddenly opened, and Hattie Mae stuck her head out.

"We're through Ms. Meadows," Hattie informed her. "You got anything else you want us to do?"

Ginger shook her head. "No, Hattie Mae. That's all for today. Thanks for your help."

"Yes, ma'am," Hattie stated with a nod. She then ducked back in the room and shouted something that the agents didn't quite catch. A second later, all of the children came racing out of the classroom. The three adults were pushed back against the wall of the vestibule as the children, screaming in delight, ran out of the building. As the last child exited the schoolhouse, the three adults reconvened their meeting.

"As I was saying," Kimble continued, "are you sure there's no one we can talk to?"

Ginger considered for a moment. "There might be one person…"

Chapter 23

A short time after meeting with Ginger Meadows, Kimble and Donnelly found themselves exiting a school for the second time that day. To Donnelly, the situation was somewhat ironic: two different schools, in different parts of town, with different student populations (White vs. Black), and yet they had pretty much ended up with the same result.

Which is nothing, Donnelly thought, but upon reflection he realized that wasn't entirely true. Ginger Meadows had given them a little more information, and a name. But time would tell if either was worthwhile in any way.

Unexpectedly, Kimble turned to his partner, asking, "So what do you think?"

"About what?" Donnelly queried in response. "You mean what she said?"

"No," Kimble replied, shaking his head and stopping for a moment. "About *her*…"

"Her?" Donnelly repeated, plainly confused as he came to a halt next to his partner – and then understanding dawned on him.

He glanced back at the school, noting that they were far enough away that any conversation they had probably couldn't be heard. Nevertheless, he whispered anyway, giving his partner an incredulous look while uttering in a low voice, "Are you kidding?"

"Come on," Kimble said in a hushed tone. "Even you must have noticed that that woman had the face of an angel, and the figure of a goddess."

"What I took note of, is the fact that she's a witness in our case," Donnelly retorted. "In fact, I'd argue she's our *primary* witness. Anything other than professional involvement with her is likely to taint this investigation."

"Who said anything about being unprofessional?" Kimble muttered. "The woman must eat, so something like dinner – even with a witness – could hardly be considered improper."

"What the hell?" Donnelly almost hissed. "Don't you ever–"

He broke off in mid-sentence as he suddenly noticed someone sitting on the hood of their car. It was Conners, the deputy sheriff. He was sitting there rolling himself a cigarette, looking so at ease that anyone would have thought he was sitting on his own vehicle.

Donnelly frowned, not liking the fact that the deputy had been that close without himself or his partner noticing. Apparently they had been too preoccupied with discussing Ginger Meadows to maintain proper awareness of their surroundings. Making eye contact with Kimble, he got the impression that his fellow agent felt the same.

The only good thing was that Conners wasn't within earshot, and on top of that the two agents had barely been speaking above a whisper. In short, it was unlikely that he had picked up on any part of their discussion. However, that didn't make either agent feel better about overlooking the presence of the deputy, who glanced up as they began walking towards him.

"Evening, gents," Conners said with a smile when they drew close.

"Deputy," Kimble replied in greeting. "To what do we owe the pleasure?"

Conners finished rolling his cigarette, then spent a moment looking it over before putting it in his mouth.

"Not pleasure," he remarked. "Business."

Kimble raised an eyebrow as Conners lit his cigarette with a match.

"See," Conners continued, "you been asking some questions that nobody around here feels like answering."

"And that makes you nervous?" Donnelly asked.

Conners shook his head. "Not me, but there are some people around here who don't like it. That's why the sheriff wants to meet with you, to talk it over."

Donnelly looked at him askance. "So why didn't he come himself and ask us?"

"He's kinda tied up right now," the deputy told them. "But he definitely wants to talk to you."

"Well Trevor, I don't think it would hurt us to spend a few minutes talking to the sheriff," Kimble suggested. "It kind of shows professional courtesy."

"That's what I'm talkin' 'bout: professional courtesy," Conners remarked, getting off their car. "Just follow me back and we'll get everything cleared up as quick and easy as fallin' off a log."

"Or a bike," Donnelly added.

Conners turned to look at him, then laughed uproariously.

Chapter 24

The sheriff's office was small and Spartan by almost any standard. It was perhaps three hundred square feet in size, with furniture that mostly consisted of a couple of aging desks and about a half-dozen rickety wooden chairs. The back wall was comprised of three holding cells, all without windows and currently unoccupied.

The sheriff's desk sat near a side wall with a hanging gun rack behind it. In truth, the gun rack – which contained a pair of rifles and a shotgun – appeared to be the only item of furniture in the office that was well-maintained. The sheriff himself was seated at the desk when Conners escorted the two agents inside.

"Hey, Zeke," the deputy called out. "Here's them two fellas you wanted to talk to."

Sheriff Washburn rose and came from around the desk, extending a hand.

"Ezekiel Washburn," he said, introducing himself. "Everybody calls me Zeke."

The two agents shook the proffered hand, introducing themselves in turn.

"Billy Kimble."

"Trevor Donnelly."

"Nice to meet you both," the sheriff told them. He then turned to his deputy. "Will, I need to speak to these boys alone for a minute."

"Huh?" mumbled Conners, looking confused. "But I thought–"

"I can handle it," the sheriff interjected, cutting him off. "Now go on down to Riley's and get yourself a drink. Tell him to put it on my tab."

Conners simply stood there for a moment, looking a bit flummoxed, then turned and left without a word. Sheriff Washburn watched him go, then shook his head in dismay.

"He's a good boy, Will is, but a mite slow to pick up on some things," the sheriff explained. "Anyway, why don't you fellas have a seat?"

As he finished speaking, Washburn motioned towards two chairs in front of his desk. Kimble and Donnelly sat down while the sheriff went back to his chair behind the desk.

"Well, you asked that we come see you," Kimble remarked. "What can we do for you?"

"It isn't so much what you can do for *me*, as it is what we can do for each other," Washburn replied.

Kimble's brow crinkled. "I'm not sure I understand."

The sheriff leaned back in his chair. "Well, you boys are here looking for Susie. Seeing as how I'm her daddy, I was thinking you'd come talk to me first."

"That was our intention," Donnelly explained, "but your deputy made it clear that you didn't want to talk to us."

Washburn sighed. "I think Will mistook what I said. What I actually told him was, it would probably be a waste of your time to talk to me."

"And why is that?" inquired Kimble.

"Because I don't know anything more than you do," the sheriff replied. "But I honestly believe that my little girl's dead."

Donnelly gave him a stern look. "Is that why you haven't tried to find her?"

"I haven't tried to find her because anything that's happened to her is no worse than she deserves," Washburn countered. "I loved her to death, but Susie flaunted the law, and I believe she paid the price."

"I know it's not popular," Kimble noted, "but I don't recall a law banning anyone from falling in love with Blacks. Plenty of laws against *marrying* them, but not falling head-over-heels for them."

"You're talking about Man's law," the sheriff declared. "I'm talking about GOD's. See, that's how the world operates – the good LORD touched us all at birth and gave us certain gifts. Just like HE blessed the three of us by making us White, HE also cursed the niggers and made them Black. By HIS law, we're superior over them, and as their superiors we need to remain separate. Susie didn't abide by that, and has probably received a just punishment as a reward."

"And Jaspar Johnson?" asked Kimble. "Did he receive a just punishment?"

Sheriff Washburn reflected for a moment. "The Tower of Babel was struck down because its builders tried to be GOD's equals...they tried to rise above their station. GOD set the example for us then; it's our duty to follow it now."

"So in your book, Jasper was punished for going above his station, and Susie *should* have been punished for going below hers," Donnelly summarized. "Is all of that your way of saying your daughter's dead?"

"What I'm saying is that if she is, it's GOD's will, and there's nothing to be gained by you trying to find her," the sheriff insisted. "Jaspar got what he had coming, and if the same has happened to Susie, then so be it! There are certain powers in the world that have to be obeyed, forces that we have to bow down to."

Donnelly's eyes narrowed. "And I suppose one of those powers is you?"

"For a man in my position, yes," Washburn grumbled with a nod, apparently getting vexed. "The people in this community trust me to keep law and order here, which you're not allowing me to do." Leaning forward, he eyed the two agents angrily. "You're coming into our home with dogshit on your shoes and tracking it all over the house – making a mess and stinking up the place. Everything was fine until you showed up, so I'd appreciate it if you'd move on as soon as possible."

"And I assume that's the real reason you wanted to see us," Kimble surmised. "Not to talk about Susie or help our investigation, but to get us to move on."

"Pretty much," the sheriff admitted.

"I'm afraid we can't do that," Kimble replied. "Sorry to have wasted your time." Turning to his partner, he added, "Come on, Trevor."

Kimble stood up, and Donnelly followed suit. At that juncture, the sheriff quickly came from behind his desk and looked Kimble in the eye.

"Now I'm real sorry to hear that," he stated. "Because it's usually best to let sleeping dogs lie, ya know. I really think that would have been best, because otherwise...well, anything can happen, and it can happen to anybody." He then repeated in a dire and ominous tone, "*Anybody.*"

"Anybody, huh?" Kimble noted, taking the veiled threat in stride. "I guess that means you, too."

The two agents then departed, with the sheriff scowling at them in silence.

Chapter 25

Exiting Zeke Washburn's office, Kimble and Donnelly began walking towards their car.

"So, what do you think of the local sheriff?" Donnelly asked.

"Not much," Kimble admitted. "But something he said…"

He trailed off and then actually came to a halt in front of a clothing store that was next to the sheriff's office. The store had a huge glass display window, and inside Kimble noticed a young Black woman – plainly an employee – putting a dress on a mannequin.

"Wait here for a minute," he told Donnelly, who had stopped walking in tandem with his partner.

Donnelly then watched, completely puzzled, as his colleague dashed inside the clothing store and began speaking to the woman. At first she seemed nervous, but then visibly relaxed. A moment later, she began speaking to Kimble while making a few pointing gestures with her hands. Kimble then gave her a brief nod and left, joining his partner outside a few moments later.

"What was that all about?" asked Donnelly.

"I'll tell you in the car," Kimble answered.

****

The two agents rode in silence, with Kimble behind the wheel. After leaving the clothing shop, he and Donnelly had gone straight to their car and driven away. In the fifteen minutes since, Donnelly had waited patiently for his partner to explain where they were headed, but Kimble had seemingly been lost in his own thoughts and thus had failed to provide any details.

"Mind telling me where we're going?" Donnelly finally asked.

"To see someone we should have talked to earlier," Kimble replied.

"And who would that be?"

"The good Reverend Thomas Bridge."

Donnelly frowned. "Who?"

Rather than answer directly, Kimble stated, "Something the sheriff mentioned back there got me thinking. Remember what he said about being in power?"

Donnelly nodded. "Yeah."

"Well, he was right to a certain extent," Kimble noted. "With him having power and a position of authority, we can pretty much forget about getting any cooperation from the White community. But let me ask you this: who's generally the most powerful person in the *Black* community?"

"No idea," Donnelly confessed with a shrug as they pulled up to a small house set on farmland, parking next to an aging red sedan. Cornstalks fully seven feet tall started a few yards from the rear of the house and extended several hundred feet.

"The preacher," Kimble told him. "Unless you're from the south like I am, you probably don't know, but the preacher is one of - if not *the* - most powerful people in the Black community. They live and breathe by what he tells them."

At that point the agents got out of the car and began approaching the house. En route to the front door, they passed a small mailbox with a name painted on it in crooked letters:

REV. T. BRIDGE

"Of course," Kimble continued, "it makes sense if you think about it. Blacks have been calling on the LORD since they were slaves – and things aren't much better for them now – so it only makes sense that the best person to rouse them up for a cause is a man of GOD."

"Well, I still think we should have talked to this guy Ginger gave us…" Donnelly said, trailing off as he checked his notepad. "…Ross Johnson. Especially since he was Jaspar's cousin."

Kimble shook his head in disgust as they stepped onto the porch. "It won't do us any good if he won't talk to us. That's why we're *here.* If we can get the good reverend on our side, maybe he can convince these people to give us some information we can work with."

As he finished speaking, Kimble rapped loudly on the door, calling out, "Reverend Bridge?"

There was no immediate response, prompting Kimble to continue knocking and shout for the good reverend again. As before, there was no answer from inside.

Kimble glanced back at the sedan they had parked next to. "He should be here. According to the girl at the shop, that's his car."

"Hmmm," Donnelly mused. Stepping away from the door, he walked to a nearby window. Putting a hand up to minimize the glare from the glass, he peeked inside.

He saw what appeared to be a cozy living room, but before he could note it in detail, an interior door opened and a man came out. As expected, he was Black, but also large – clearly overweight. Presumably, the room he had come from was a bedroom, because the man was half-naked. Grabbing a pair of pants from the floor, he hurriedly shoved a leg into them, then hopped around for a second while trying to get into the other pants leg.

Turning away before he was noticed, Donnelly went back to his partner, saying, "I think he's coming."

Kimble acknowledged this with a nod, but continued banging on the door anyway. "Reverend Bridge? You in there?"

"Who is it?" a masculine voice suddenly asked from the other side of the door.

"Special Agents Donnelly and Kimble with the FBI," Donnelly announced. "We'd like to speak with you."

"Just a minute," came the response.

The two agents then stood patiently as perhaps another fifteen seconds went by, and then the door was opened by the man Donnelly had spied earlier through the window – presumably, Reverend Bridge.

Getting a better look at him, Donnelly noted that he was close to middle age. However, judging from the man's antics when putting on his pants, he was seemingly still lively and spry, despite his age and size.

Breathing hard and sweating slightly, he greeted the agents with a smile. "Sorry 'bout the wait. Won't you come in?"

Upon receiving the invitation, the agents went inside and found themselves in the living room that Donnelly had observed through the window earlier, although now he could see it in more detail. The furniture was old – as were the appliances in a nearby kitchen – but everything looked clean and well-kept. He also noted a large chocolate cake (with a thick slice missing) sitting on a nearby table. Outside a nearby window they could see the field of corn.

"I hope we weren't disturbing you," Kimble said.

Reverend Bridge shook his head, "Not at all. I was just–"

He stopped abruptly as an odd sound, like something being knocked over, came from a back room of the house. More specifically, it seemed to originate from the room Donnelly had seen the reverend exit from earlier.

"Is someone else here?" Donnelly asked as he headed towards the room in question.

"No, it's just me," Bridge said as Donnelly, with his partner and the reverend right behind him, opened the door to the room.

The agents found themselves staring at a modest bedroom, which contained a dresser-and-mirror, as well as a chifferobe. The main feature of the room, of course, was a full-sized bed that currently had ruffled sheets – as though someone had only just gotten out of it minutes ago. There was also a nightstand next to the bed, and on the floor next to it was a small lamp. Presumably it was the lamp that had fallen, but – surprisingly – it hadn't broken.

Donnelly and Kimble both took all this in with a glance. However, what really drew their attention was a window next to the nightstand. It was currently open, and through it they could see a young girl dashing towards the cornfield. She glanced back towards the house as she ran, and Donnelly was surprised to see that it was Hattie Mae – the girl from the school where Ginger Meadows taught.

"Ahem," said the reverend, clearing his throat and getting his visitors' attention. "As I said, I'm here by myself and was just having a little snack while my wife's out." He then spent a moment patting his large stomach. "She wants me to lose some weight…don't approve of how much I eat."

Kimble gestured towards the chocolate cake. "Maybe you should cut out the extra sweets."

"Or the sweet sixteens," Donnelly added as Hattie Mae disappeared into the field of corn.

Reverend Bridge stared at him for a moment, then let out a deep laugh. Kimble smiled back while Donnelly simply looked at Bridge with a blank expression. A few seconds later, Bridge stopped chortling but a devilish grin remained on his face.

"Well, all have sinned and come short of the glory of GOD," the reverend noted. "What more can I say? I have vices, like everyone else. My problem is, I'm a man of large appetites, but man shall not live by bread alone - if you understand me."

"I guess he also does not sleep in bed alone," Donnelly quipped.

The reverend went into another round of uproarious laughter. Following this, he flopped down into a nearby easy chair and motioned for the two agents to take a seat on an ancient sofa across from him.

"So what can I do for you gents?" he asked.

"I'm sure you already know the answer to that," Kimble responded.

"Yep, I'm afraid I do," Bridge admitted. "It's all over town that you're asking about Susie Washburn. Not much I can tell you, though. I wasn't really acquainted with the girl. She wasn't really a sheep of my flock, you understand."

"But you must have heard something," Donnelly insisted.

"Nothing you haven't heard already," Reverend Bridge countered. "Namely, that Susie Washburn run off with Jaspar Johnson. The Klan caught up with 'em. End of story."

"So you think she's dead?" Kimble asked.

Bridge looked at him with a candid expression. "Mister, I been Black my whole life, and I can tell you from experience that if there's one thing the Klan hates more than a nigger, it's a nigger-*luvah*. Now you know 'bout what they did to Jaspar...you can guess what probably happened to *her*. But that's about all I know."

"That's about all anyone seems to know," Donnelly noted.

"Nobody wants to talk, huh?" the reverend chuckled. "I cudda told you that from the start. If I can say this without offending you gents, you're wasting your time. Nobody in this town is gonna get themselves killed trying to help you. It ain't worth it. Even if it *was* worth it, nobody in this town has the guts to try."

"We were told there might be somebody..." Kimble hinted, trailing off.

Reverend Bridge's eyebrows rose in surprise. "Who?"

"Ross Johnson," Donnelly said. "He's supposed to be Jaspar's cousin."

The reverend was silent for a moment, then burst out laughing.

"What's so funny?" asked Donnelly.

Almost in hysterics, Reverend Bridge uttered, "Have you...have you...have you *seen* Ross Johnson yet?"

The agents looked at each other, then Kimble answered, "No, why?"

Still laughing, the reverend said, "No…no…no reason!"

The agents shared another glance, then waited patiently until Bridge's mirth subsided.

As his laughter eventually died, the reverend seemed to nod to himself and then stated, "Yeah, I suppose Ross just might talk to you after all. Boy, I wish I could be there for that!"

"And why, exactly, is that?" Kimble inquired.

Rather than respond, Reverend Bridge exploded into another round of hysterical laughter.

Chapter 26

Neither Donnelly nor Kimble spoke much on the ride back to town. Once there, Donnelly – who was driving – brought their vehicle to a halt in front of the town's general store.

"Well, this is it," stated Kimble. "According to Ginger, that's where Ross Johnson works."

"Ginger?" Donnelly repeated. "One short meeting and you're already on a first-name basis with her?"

"Well, like you said, she's our witness," Kimble reminded him. "A certain level of informality may help her feel comfortable with us."

"She seemed comfortable enough," Donnelly noted. "No need to roll out the welcome wagon any further."

Kimble gave a noncommittal grunt in response, then spent a moment looking over the general store.

Like a number of other buildings in Evangeline, it was plainly antiquated, but not decrepit. It was well-preserved, which suggested that someone regularly performed repairs and maintenance – at least on the exterior, although presumably the interior was the same.

Looking at it, Donnelly began to reflect on the person they were there to speak with.

"What do you suppose it is about this guy that had the good reverend in stitches like that?" he asked his partner.

"Don't know," Kimble confessed, shaking his head. "Maybe he shits gold."

"Oh, now that's beautiful…practically poetry," Donnelly said. "You come up with that yourself?"

Kimble just looked at him and smiled. Shaking his head in disdain, Donnelly prepared to get out of the car, but he suddenly noticed that Kimble hadn't moved.

Donnelly gave him a curious look. "Aren't we going to go in?"

"For what?" Kimble replied. "It's too late to go see him today."

"How do you figure?"

"I'm from a small town like this, remember?" Kimble said. "Soon as the sun sets, people close shop and go home for the night. We may as well do the same."

"Okay, I guess that makes sense," Donnelly admitted.

"Of course it does," Kimble crowed. "Besides, there's a sign in the window that says 'Closed.'

****

Unable to talk to the next person on their list, the agents grabbed a quick bite to eat and then retired for the evening.

However, just like the night before, Kimble slipped out of bed at a late hour and swiftly – but quietly – dressed while Donnelly slept. He then departed.

As Kimble left the room, Donnelly slowly opened his eyes. He quickly sat up and looked around. Taking a peek out the window, he saw Kimble get into the passenger side of a waiting truck and drive off.

"What the hell?" Donnelly muttered, plainly perplexed. That said, he lay down again and managed to fall back asleep rather easily.

The next morning, his partner was back in bed as though nothing had happened. As before, though, when

Kimble finally opened his eyes, he discovered that Donnelly was already dressed and awake.

Kimble squinted in the morning light. "Is there some particular reason why you get up this early every day?"

"Can't seem to help it," Donnelly told him. "After a good night's sleep, I just wake up ready to go."

"Yeah, I noticed that you sleep like a log for most of the night."

"And I noticed that you *don't*," Donnelly shot back.

"Huh?" muttered Kimble, giving him an odd look.

"Well, it's just that I woke up around midnight last night and you were gone," Donnelly explained.

"Uh, yeah," Kimble muttered a bit uneasily, sitting up. "Well, I tend to get a little restless sometimes, so I'll get up and go for a walk. It relaxes me a bit and helps me get back to sleep."

"Oh," Donnelly muttered with a slight bit of skepticism.

"Anyway," Kimble droned, "give me a few minutes to get ready, and we can go see this Ross Johnson guy."

Although he had more questions about his partner's late-night antics, Donnelly merely nodded, deciding he'd address the issue in full at a later time.

Chapter 27

The two agents actually didn't go directly from their hotel room to the general store. Instead, they got breakfast first, consisting of coffee and sweet rolls from the bakery Donnelly had visited the day before. It wasn't a well-balanced meal, but it was definitely delicious. The town may have had its drawbacks, but pastries clearly weren't one of them.

Afterwards, they made their way to the general store. They encountered only a few townspeople en route, but those they did gave them a wide berth – with at least one person going so far as to cross to the other side of the street to avoid them.

"Should I be offended?" Donnelly asked as they walked.

"What, you don't care for southern hospitality?" Kimble joked with a grin.

"If this is hospitality," Donnelly quipped, "I can't imagine what *inhospitable* must look like."

Kimble chuckled. "Well, like the sheriff said, we're tracking dogshit through the homes of these good people. They're just counting the minutes until we're gone."

Donnelly let out a snort of disdain. "Based on the reception we've received thus far, dogshit is probably an improvement."

Kimble laughed aloud at the comment, causing a few heads to turn in their direction. At that point, they had reached the store. Contrary to the prior evening, the sign in the window now read "Open." Taking that as his cue, Donnelly opened the door and entered, followed by his partner.

As the agents stepped inside the general store, a bell above the door jingled loudly, blatantly announcing their presence. The interior was small but well-stocked, with a variety of goods lining shelves on both the walls and a couple of center-aisles. Next to the door was a small counter on which there sat a cash register and a few books. Near the rear, they could see a young man, tall and blond-haired, taking cans out of a box and stacking them on a shelf.

Not seeing anyone else, they walked towards him, but the man – presumably a store clerk or employee, based on the apron he wore – continued working with his back to them and never even turned in their direction. The agents halted a few feet from him.

"Excuse me," Kimble began, "we're looking for Ross Johnson. We understand he works here."

"Yes, he does," the clerk confirmed in a crisp, clear tone, although he still didn't turn around.

Kimble and Donnelly simply stood there, obviously expecting the clerk to expound on his statement. However, after a few seconds it became clear that wasn't going to happen, as the clerk just kept stocking the shelves with his back to them.

The two agents exchanged a glance, then Kimble stated, "Well, like I said, we're looking for him."

"If I can get you to change that preposition you used from 'for' to 'at,'" the clerk responded, "I can probably make you a happy man."

"Huh?" muttered Kimble.

At that point, the young man finally turned to face them. Donnelly noted that he was handsome, with piercing blue eyes, and appeared to be in his early twenties.

"You said you're looking for Ross Johnson," the young man noted. "Well, you're no longer looking *for* him; you're looking *at* him."

Donnelly and Kimble simply stared at him in confusion for a moment.

"No, no, no," Kimble said after a few seconds. "There's obviously been some mistake. The Ross Johnson we're looking for–"

"– is Black," the clerk – Ross – interjected. "Yes, I know. And here I am."

Donnelly looked him up and down for a moment, plainly trying to wed what he was hearing to what he was seeing.

Apparently throwing in the towel after a few seconds, he blurted out, "But you're not Black!"

Chapter 28

"You're not *Black*," Donnelly repeated, as if trying to convince himself. "You're *White*."

Ross sighed. "I suppose, Agent Donnelly, that someone should have explained to you that 'Black' in this instance is defined by pedigree, not pigmentation. Therefore, by virtue of being of African descent, I am classified as Black – despite the fact that my blood is at least three-quarters White. As far as the good people of Evangeline are concerned – more specifically, the good *White* people – I might as well be black as coal."

Ross then went back to stacking cans on the shelves.

"You called him Agent Donnelly," Kimble noted. "That means you already know who we are."

Ross gave him a solemn look. "The gators and the rats are the only creatures within miles that don't know who you are, Agent Kimble…or why you're here. Anybody who says anything different is not being truthful."

Kimble took that in with a nod. "We were told you might be able to help us."

"Any number of people in this town are *able* to help you," Ross noted derisively. "What you need is someone who's *willing* to do so."

Donnelly looked at him askance. "Are you saying that you won't?"

"What I'm saying is that there's a calculated risk involved in helping you," Ross clarified. "And I'm not entirely sure that the risk is worth the reward – whatever that may be."

"I would think that of all the people in this town, you'd be the one most willing to help," Donnelly admonished. "After all, it was your cousin who got killed."

"Well, are you here to investigate his murder?" Ross inquired. "If so, that definitely changes how I feel about helping you, because right now my natural inclination is to stay uninvolved. So tell me: are you here to investigate Jaspar's death?"

Kimble shook his head. "No, but we know that he was involved in our case somehow, and that it got him killed."

"I'm well aware of that fact," Ross informed them, "and I've developed a particular aversion to ending up that way myself. Did they tell you how he died?"

"Not in detail," Kimble confessed.

"Well, allow me to enlighten you," Ross said. "First, he was dismembered – most notably, they cut off his hands to punish him for touching a White woman. Next, they castrated him, to make sure that a particular offense would never be repeated. Finally, they took a knife and carved the words 'Good Nigger' in his back – the analogy, of course, being that the only good nigger is a dead nigger. Then they set him on fire."

As Ross had given the gory details of his cousin's murder, Donnelly had gone from appearing ill-at-ease to wan, and then finally to looking physically ill. Kimble looked fairly uncomfortable as well.

"Believe me, we're terribly sorry to hear that," Kimble stressed. "But the reason we're here is to find Susie."

A disgusted expression settled on Ross's face. "I can't help but find it amazing. This entire town has been struck dumb on the subject of a missing White girl, but everyone muses freely on the torture and murder of a Black man. The men who did it basically brag about it."

Kimble stepped forward and put a sympathetic hand on his shoulder.

"Look," Kimble remarked, "I didn't know Jaspar, but I'm sorry for him and the way he died. That shouldn't happen to a dog. But we can't do anything for him. Maybe we can do something for Susie, though, and we could use your help."

Ross looked at him with watery eyes. "What do you want to know?"

"Anything you can tell us," Kimble replied.

Chapter 29

Ross crossed his arms and lowered his head in thought.

"Jaspar started working for the sheriff roughly a year ago," he began. "He was really happy about the employment and it brought him into close contact with Susie. Surprisingly, they were a lot alike."

"How's that?" asked Donnelly, who had his pad out and was taking notes.

"For one thing, they both lost their mothers at a young age," Ross replied. "Jaspar's mother – my mother's sister – died in childbirth, so Jaspar and I were raised like brothers. Anyway, I assume that having lost their mothers was the first step he and Susie took towards bonding, and as for the rest, I guess nature took its course."

"You're saying that they were lovers," Kimble concluded.

"I'm sure you've already developed a theory concerning the nature of their relationship," Ross remarked. "I don't think you need me to confirm it."

Kimble gave Ross an odd look. "Do you always talk like this?"

"No, occasionally I drop down on all fours and communicate through a series of grunts and growls," Ross blurted out sarcastically. He then walked towards the front of the store, with the two agents following.

"What's the matter, Agent Kimble?" Ross continued. "Is the use of proper English and diction by a Negro outside your realm of experience? Well, it may also shock you to know that I also walk upright, and have a tendency to use utensils when I eat."

Ross stopped in front of a large metal door set in the wall. Opening it, he stepped inside what appeared to be a walk-in freezer.

Kimble called in after him, saying, "I just wanted to compliment you. You seem very articulate."

Ross exited the freezer carrying a large slab of meat. He closed the door with his leg before stepping to a scale on a nearby counter.

Placing the meat on the scale, he said, "Articulate for a Black man, you mean."

Kimble shook his head as Ross reached beneath the counter and pulled out an empty sack labeled "FLOUR".

"No," Kimble insisted. "I just meant in general."

Ross placed the meat in the sack. Kimble and Donnelly watched him suspiciously, wondering what he was doing.

"Then why mention it?" demanded Ross. "If I were a White man and spoke as I do, would you feel the need to compliment me on my pattern of speech?" Neither agent answered, prompting Ross to add, "I thought not…"

He then grabbed the sack of meat and walked to the rear of the store. The agents followed, noting that he entered a small storage room full of boxes. At the back of the room, however, was a door. Ross set the sack on the floor and opened the rear door, which led outside. He stuck his head out and glanced around, then – leaving the door open – turned back to face the two agents.

"Look, I didn't mean anything by what I said," Kimble insisted. "It's just that I don't often hear many people, White or Black, talk like you."

"I realize that," Ross stated, "but I despise being looked upon as an exception due to the fact that it demeans the rest of the Black race."

Donnelly frowned in confusion. "I'm afraid I don't follow you."

"To most Caucasians, I am physically representative of a White man," Ross explained. "Upon learning my true nature, however, they will concede me my merits - such as my articulation and intelligence - but it's all attributed to being the result of having a White father. They assume that a person born of two Negro parents would not be quite as bright, and that is what you imply when you compliment me in such a manner. It would be far better for the race as a whole if a person of a darker hue had received the gifts that have been bestowed upon me."

Before Kimble or Donnelly could respond, there was a light knock near the back door. All three men looked in the direction of the sound and saw Bobby, Luthor's son, outside with a small red wagon and a look of uncertainty on his face. Ross gave him a huge smile before racing over and picking him up, lifting him high into the air.

"Hey there Bobby, buddy!" Ross exclaimed congenially. "Whatcha doin' here, huh?"

Kimble and Donnelly found themselves amazed at the change in Ross's speech and demeanor. Meanwhile, Bobby giggled in delight as Ross repeatedly tossed him up and caught him before finally putting him down. At that point, Bobby reached into a pocket and pulled out some coins.

"Got something for me, huh?" asked Ross.

Bobby nodded as he handed the coins over. "Mama said to get some flour."

"Flour, huh?" Ross mused as he began counting the money. "Let's see...nine cents. Flour is three cents a pound, so that's three pounds. Let's see if I've got any."

Ross looked around for a moment before picking up the slab of meat in the flour bag. Kimble cocked an eyebrow at Donnelly, but both continued watching in silence as Ross placed the bag into Bobby's wagon along with another sack of flour that presumably contained the real thing.

"Alright, that should do it," Ross announced. "Tell your mama that I hope Luthor gets better soon."

"Okay," Booby said as he waved goodbye and began pulling the wagon away.

Going back inside, Ross found the two agents looking at him in an odd way. However, he ignored their expressions as he closed and locked the door.

He then turned to his visitors. "Now, where were we?"

"I was just wondering what your accountant says when he sees your books," Kimble commented.

"Nothing," Ross declared, "because I feel that talking to myself is a bad habit."

"So you're the accountant?" Queried Donnelly. "And the owner trusts you?"

"The owner?" Ross repeated, sounding amused. "Ostensibly, I *am* the owner. Legally, however, the store belongs to one Ross Michaels, Sr."

"Ross Michaels?" Kimble uttered, eyes going wide. "*The* Ross Michaels?"

Ross nodded.

Donnelly, clearly not following the discussion, asked, "Who's Ross Michaels?"

Chapter 30

For a moment it looked as though no one was going to answer Donnelly's question, then his partner spoke up.

"Ross Michaels," Kimble explained, "is a rich old coot who owns almost all the land in three states...one of the richest men south of the Mason-Dixon line and part of an old Quaker family."

"He's also my grandfather," Ross added.

"What?" Kimble muttered incredulously.

"His initial desire was to give me the store, but I said 'No,'" Ross continued. "The Whites in this town wouldn't allow a Negro to have his own business, so nominally the store still belongs to my grandfather, as does the old family mansion on the outskirts of town. For all intents and purposes, however, they belong to me. The store I find useful; the mansion I do not – particularly since it was burned down."

"Hold on for a second," Kimble stated. "Ross Michaels is really your grandfather?"

"He is," Ross confirmed.

"But how?" Kimble almost demanded.

"My father was his son," Ross replied. "His *only* son. He died in a train wreck when I was six. Somewhere along the way, word got back to Ross Senior that, aside from his three legitimate daughters, Ross Junior also had a son with a Creole woman who was growing up to be the spitting image of his father. He came to visit, and for some odd reason he developed a natural affinity for me. When I was twelve, he hired a man named Finley to run this store and made me Finley's clerk. Finley was allowed to keep all the profits in return for fulfilling the duties of his *real* job."

"Which was what?" inquired Donnelly.

"Tutoring me," Ross explained. "You see, my grandfather's family has lived in these parts for quite some time, and he understood better than anyone what would happen if the Whites in this town knew that I was being raised to be smarter than their own children. Therefore, Finley – under the pretext of being my boss – was actually tutoring me in all the subjects that you gentlemen probably took for granted. After my tutelage, Finley moved on and the store was given into my charge."

"What about Jaspar?" asked Kimble. "Did he get tutored, too?"

"No," Ross answered, shaking his head. "My grandfather probably would have been okay with it, but Jaspar had…other ambitions."

"Involving Susie?" Kimble guessed.

"Some of them, yes, but much of that came later," Ross responded. "And as complicated as things were initially with Susie, they got even worse."

Donnelly looked at him with a curious expression. "How?"

"She was pregnant when they disappeared," Ross declared.

"What?" Kimble blurted out in shock.

"How do you know?" asked Donnelly. "Did one of them tell you?"

"No one had to tell me," Ross said. "I'm the only store in town."

Kimble frowned. "I don't think I follow you."

"After they reach a certain age, women have certain hygienical needs," Ross noted. "Being the only source of the necessary items, I'm often the first to know, by inference you understand, when a woman in this town is expecting."

"How does that work?" queried Donnelly. "They just come in and tell you what they need?"

"Hardly," Ross responded. "This is not a topic that women are comfortable discussing with men – or even other females outside their own families. So no, they don't tell me anything. We have a catalog, and they order what they need from it. The items arrive wrapped and sealed for privacy purposes, and I simply hold them until the buyers come pick them up. However I should clarify: not all the women in town use commercially available sanitary products. Some use other methods, or homemade remedies."

"But Susie was one of those who ordered hygiene products through you," Donnelly surmised.

"She did," Ross confirmed. "Until she didn't..."

"So Susie was, in your opinion, expecting?" Donnelly asked.

"By virtue of the facts at my disposal, yes," Ross stated.

Kimble, whose head had been lowered in thought for a few seconds, suddenly looked up."

"Well, I think that's all we need right now," he remarked. "Come on, Trevor."

Donnelly looked as though he had more to discuss with Ross, but instead chose to follow his partner's lead. Ergo, the agents thanked Ross for his time and then headed for the exit.

Looking back at Ross, Kimble added, "If we need anything else, we'll be in touch."

With that, Donnelly opened the door and prepared to step out. However, he bumped into an elderly Black woman who was just coming in.

"Excuse me," Donnelly apologized, at the same time reaching out a hand to help steady the woman.

Something the woman was cradling in her hands unexpectedly snapped at his fingers. It was a baby alligator.

Donnelly snatched his hand back in alarm, at the same time staggering backwards until he tripped over a box that was behind him.

"Holy shit!" Donnelly uttered, drawing his gun. However, before he could take any further action, Kimble put a hand on his wrist.

"Easy there, kid," his partner coaxed. "It's just a baby."

The little alligator hissed softly as the old woman stroked it. She was dressed in dirty, tattered clothing and muttering something unintelligible under her breath as she stared at Donnelly. Ross hurriedly stepped between the old woman and the agent.

"It's okay," Ross stressed. "This is Mama Lu...she's harmless."

Donnelly, who was just being helped to his feet by Kimble, gave him a hard stared, saying, "Well what about that thing in her arms?"

"It's not big enough to harm anything more than a lizard," Ross insisted. Turning to mama Lu, he said, "Go on in the back, now. I'll be there in a minute. Go on."

He gave her a slight push in the right direction. Mama Lu walked past Donnelly with an evil look in her eye, still muttering.

"You'll have to forgive old Mama Lu," Ross told them. "She's lived out in the swamps longer than most people in this town have been alive. Her mind isn't as sharp as it once was, but she has a will of iron."

"Any more nuts like that live around here?" asked Donnelly.

Ross's eyes narrowed. "No, but we occasionally get one or two from out of town."

Interjecting before his partner could say anything, Kimble remarked, "Well, like I said, we'll be in touch if we need anything else."

He then hustled his partner out of the store.

Chapter 31

The two agents walked away from the store, with Donnelly still dumbfounded by what had just happened inside.

"A pet alligator!" he uttered as they headed towards their car. "Tell me, is that the weirdest thing you've ever seen?"

"Does a bear shit in the woods?" Kimble muttered as they reached their vehicle. "Look kid, if you're in this business any length of time, you see all kinds of things that people do. But to be honest, I found Ross Johnson almost as interesting as that baby gator. I think I see why Reverend Bridge reacted the way he did when we mentioned him."

"Speaking of the good reverend," Donnelly said as they got into the car, "do we need to do anything about him?"

"Anything like what?"

"He had that girl in his bedroom," Donnelly replied. "And we don't have to guess what he was doing with her."

"Maybe, but why bring it up now? All that happened yesterday. Did it suddenly start bothering you?"

"It's actually been bothering me since we left him," Donnelly stated truthfully. "You mentioning him again just brought it back to mind."

"Well, let's think about it: what did we actually see? I mean, did either of us actually *see* her in his bedroom?"

"No," Donnelly admitted almost reluctantly.

"Did we even see her inside the house?"

"No, but she knocked that lamp over while slipping out the window."

"There's also a plausible argument that she knocked it over while maybe trying to break in and steal something, then got scared and ran off."

Donnelly opened his mouth as if to say something, then closed it again.

"Also," Kimble continued, "how old would you say that girl was?"

"I don't know," Donnelly admitted with a shrug. "Sixteen, seventeen…"

"That's about what I thought, too," Kimble noted. "Now, do you know what the age of consent is in Louisiana?"

Donnelly shook his head. "No."

"Well I do: it's seventeen. See, my mother had an older cousin who was from here. Care to guess what the age of consent was when she was growing up?"

"What?" asked Donnelly.

"Twelve."

"What the hell?" muttered Donnelly, frowning. "You're kidding, right?"

"Nope," Kimble replied. "And it wasn't just Louisiana – that was the age of consent in a bunch of states. It kind of explains how my mom's cousin ended up married at fourteen and having her first kid a year later."

Donnelly didn't say anything, but still didn't look convinced.

"Look," Kimble went on, "I'm not saying your thinking is out of line. I'm just pointing out that we're a long way from being able to even assert that a crime *occurred*, let alone prove it."

"Even so, shouldn't we tell somebody what we saw? What we suspect?"

"Tell who – the sheriff? Do you honestly think he gives a shit what happens on that side of the color line?"

"Not really," Donnelly admitted. "But the Black folks around here might care."

"Except that's not why we're here. And even if we did tell somebody our suspicions, Reverend Bridge will just say we're White devils spreading lies. And who do you think the Blacks in this town will believe?"

"So what are you saying – that we should just do nothing?"

Kimble looked at Donnelly in exasperation. His partner clearly wasn't letting this go.

"Alright," Kimble finally muttered. "It seems to me the threshold question is the girl's age. What say we figure that out first, and then we can decide if we need to do anything else, okay?"

"Sounds reasonable," Donnelly stated with a nod.

"Good," Kimble said flatly. "You know what would also be good? If we got back to working on the case we're actually investigating."

"Fine," Donnelly said. "Any new ideas in that regard?"

"Yeah," Kimble remarked, nodding. "Something Ross said while we were in the store got me thinking. Maybe we're attacking this thing from the wrong angle."

"What do you mean?"

"What I mean is that Susie Washburn's disappearance is why we're here, right? Now, we know that she and Jaspar disappeared together, but then he turns up dead and she can't be found."

"So?"

"Well, no one in this town wants to talk about Susie. But just like Ross said, they don't seem to care when it comes to talking about Jaspar. So since we know the two of them were together, maybe if we focus our attention on Jaspar's murder, we can find out what happened to Susie."

Donnelly seemed to consider that for a moment. "It's worth a try, but where do we start?"

"Well, let's consider," Kimble proposed. "Where around here could you hide for six months and not be seen by anyone?"

"Relatives?" Donnelly suggested.

Kimble shook his head. "First place they'd look if someone's searching for you. But let's assume that you don't want to be seen by *anyone* – including family. What's left?"

"Definitely not the swamps – not after what Merrill Wright told us."

"True," Kimble agreed.

"Maybe in some farmer's barn or shed, or a deserted house, or–"

"That's it!" Kimble exclaimed, snapping his fingers.

Excited, he started the car and then the two of them drove off.

Chapter 32

Once again, Donnelly and Kimble found themselves traveling down a dirt road. In Donnelly's mind, it was almost the only type of thoroughfare Evangeline had, although at least on this occasion the scenery was slightly different, with wheat growing on both sides of the roadway.

"So, where are we going?" Donnelly asked.

"Do you remember those abandoned houses we saw before?" his partner inquired.

"Yeah," Donnelly assured him with a nod.

"Well, those were actually slave quarters. A hundred years ago, all of this land you see here was part of a plantation worked by slaves."

"And you know this how?"

Kimble paused for a second. "Remember when I mentioned going out for a walk last night?"

"Sure."

"Well, our lovely landlady was waiting for me when I came back. Apparently she's got ears like a bat and heard me leave. My guess is that she thought I was going to try to smuggle a woman in, because she seemed disappointed at not catching me red-handed in some way. Anyway, I took the opportunity to try to sweet talk her, convince her that I wasn't that type of guy."

"How'd that work out for you?"

"She wasn't buying it. But when I expressed interest in the town she did tell me a little of the history – including some interesting tidbits about local slave owners."

As he finished speaking, Kimble pulled to a stop in front of several old, abandoned buildings. They were wooden structures, made from lumber that looked dark and decrepit. Undaunted, the two agents stepped out of the car and approach one of the buildings.

"So, did she say what happened here?" Donnelly asked. "Why people just abandoned these places?"

"No, but she didn't have to," Kimble replied as he tapped the porch of the building with his foot, testing the wood before stepping onto it.

"Huh?" muttered his partner, following him.

"Don't they teach you kids History anymore?" Kimble asked, shaking his head in mock disdain. "Honest Abe freed the slaves."

As he finished speaking they entered the building (which didn't have a door), with the old wood creaking loudly under their feet. They found themselves in a small cabin with two rooms. The place was littered with trash and debris, as well as rats and vermin that squeaked and scattered as they came inside.

"After they were free," Kimble continued, "some of the former slaves got the hell away from the South. Others stayed, but they moved out of these old places."

"I can see why," Donnelly commented as they advanced towards the second room. "I can't imagine anyone living in a place like this."

"It's not like they had a choice," his partner observed. "See, that's the concept behind slavery. They – ahhhhh!"

Kimble's statement became a yelp as he crashed through rotting wood that came up to his thighs.

"Holy shit!" Donnelly blurted out. "Are you okay?"

"Does a fish have titties?" Kimble demanded. "Hell no, I'm not okay! Help me out of here!"

Laughing, Donnelly reached down with a hand to help his partner.

****

Kimble exited from a cabin and began dusting his hands off just as Donnelly emerged from another. Kimble called to him as they stepped off their respective porches and approached one another.

"Find anything?" Kimble inquired.

"No," Donnelly answered. "You?"

Kimble shook his head.

After their experience in the first cabin, they had continued searching others in the area, splitting up to make better time. Thus far, their efforts had yielded no fruit.

"We've been at this for hours," Donnelly observed in frustration. "I don't think Susie and Jaspar stayed in any of these places. These cabins are all on their last legs. They would have been safer taking their chances with the Klan than staying in one of these."

"I agree," Kimble told him, "but they never left this town, so they had to be staying somewhere. Sure as hell wasn't at the governor's mansion."

Donnelly, in the process of smacking dust from his trousers, suddenly looked up.

"What did you say?" he asked.

"What?" Kimble muttered, looking confused. "Just a joke – that they weren't staying at the governor's mansion."

Somewhat excited, Donnelly reached into his coat pocket and pulled out his notepad. Next, he began hastily flipping through it.

"Do you remember what Ross said this morning," he quizzed. "About a family mansion?"

"Yeah," Kimble responded. "He said it got burned down."

"But he also said that it was *his*. Now, do you think that his White grandfather would give the place to his Negro grandson if there was still anyone living there? So that means..."

"The place was abandoned," Kimble concluded as his partner trailed off. "Good work, kid! I mean, Trevor."

Donnelly didn't bother to respond as the two of them went racing back to their car.

Chapter 33

There weren't a lot of burned-down estates in the area, so it didn't take much effort to find the place they were looking for or identify it as the proper residence. Most of the mansion was rubble, although one wall was still standing. The rest had collapsed in the fire, with some of it having also cascaded across the yard.

Upon arrival, the two agents immediately began sifting through the burned and charred debris looking for clues. However, given how badly everything was scorched, the odds of them finding anything seemed slim, and after about fifteen minutes Kimble appeared ready to give up.

"See anything yet?" he asked Donnelly.

"Nothing but that thing over there," his partner replied, pointing to an alligator resting in the shade beneath some trees maybe a hundred feet away.

"Geez!" Kimble exclaimed, looking at the reptile. "This place is right on the edge of the fucking swamp! Who the hell puts a mansion in a place like this?"

"Didn't they teach you old codgers history when you were in school?" Donnelly teased. "These people were Quakers, remember? Quakers were known to help runaway slaves. Being located right on the edge of the swamp probably gave the slaves a better chance to escape."

"Hell, I thought that was mostly about the underground railroad – secret passages and things like that."

"You can bet there were likely a few in this place, but they're probably all gone now."

Kimble picked up a half-burned pillow and tossed it aside. "Well, I'll give you credit: looking here was definitely a good idea, but I don't think there's anything here we can use. Even if there is, it's probably burned beyond recognition."

"No, you said it yourself - an agent's instincts are sometimes better than anything else. I *know* that this is where Susie and Jaspar were. I can feel it. There's something here. There *has* to be!"

Kimble shook his head. "I'm afraid I just don't see it, Trevor. I'm not even sure this wasn't just a regular old house fire. What makes you think this is the place?"

"Just a hunch," Donnelly answered, at the same time reaching down and pulling something up from the rubble.

At first it appeared to be a long plank of wood, then Kimble suddenly recognized the object his partner had found.

"Well, I'll be damned," Kimble muttered, then just stared at what Donnelly had pulled from the debris: a charred cross – the calling card of the KKK.

****

Several hours later, Donnelly and Kimble stood at the open trunk of their car, looking solemnly at its contents – items they had recovered while searching the remains of the mansion. As a testament to their efforts, both men were covered in ash and soot.

"Is that it?" Kimble asked. "All of it?"

"Aside from the cross, yes" Donnelly answered with a nod.

Kimble looked at the articles in their trunk, then declared, "Gruesome as some of it is, it's not a whole lot of evidence."

"It'll have to do."

Seemingly in agreement, Kimble slammed the trunk shut and went around to the driver's side.

"Hey! Why is it that you always get to drive?" Donnelly demanded.

Kimble tossed him the keys and walked around to the passenger side, stating, "Makes no difference to me."

Moments later they were in the car. Donnelly started the engine and began driving.

"Since you're in the driver's seat, so to speak," Kimble noted, "what do you think our next move should be?"

"First, I'd like to get back and have a bath," Donnelly responded, "then get into some fresh clothes. After that, I suppose one of us can go ask Ms. Meadows what she knows about what we've got" – he motioned with his thumb towards the trunk of the car – "while the other goes to pay another visit to our good friend Ross Johnson."

"Well, you seem to have a pretty good handle on Ross," Kimble noted. "Why don't you take him and I'll take Ms. Meadows."

"By force, or with her consent?" Donnelly asked, giving his partner a skeptical look.

Kimble merely laughed in response.

Chapter 34

Ross Johnson was sitting behind the counter reading a book when Donnelly came into the store carrying a brown paper bag.

"Agent Donnelly," Ross began, setting the book down. "To what do I owe the pleasure?"

"Business, I'm afraid," Donnelly responded. "Not pleasure."

"Still, what can I do for you?"

"I'm interested in the Michaels family mansion. You said this morning that you owned it."

"Not precisely," Ross corrected, shaking his head. "What I said was that I am the owner for all intents and purposes. Transfer of title to my name, however, has never occurred, although my grandfather made it quite clear that the property was mine to do with as I wish. I much prefer, however, to sleep in my room above the store."

As he finished speaking, Ross pointed up with his finger.

"It's a good thing you do," Donnelly noted, "because the fire you had out there barely left anything standing."

"So I've been told," Ross remarked. "I've yet to inspect the damage myself."

"My partner and I have reason to believe that your cousin Jaspar and Susie Washburn were there – at least up until the night of the fire."

Before Ross could respond, the door opened and two young White women entered. One of them – a pretty blonde – smiled flirtatiously at Ross, who ignored the gesture and remained stone-faced as the women approached the counter. On his part, Donnelly unobtrusively stepped away to allow Ross to deal with his customers.

"Hi, Ross," said the blonde with a big grin.

"Yes, ma'am?" Ross stated in a polite but disinterested tone.

"Oh, Ross," the blonde giggled. "You don't have to call me ma'am! You can just call me Jamie."

"Yes, ma'am," Ross replied, making the blonde, Jamie, giggle again.

"We just want the usual," she told him.

"A pack of gum?" Ross inquired.

"Uh-huh," Jamie stated with a nod.

Ross immediately turned around and got a pack of gum from a rack behind him. He placed it on the counter and slid it across to Jamie, who held out some change in her hand. However, rather than reach for it, Ross merely waited.

"Well, go on – take it," Jamie insisted. "I don't bite!"

Reluctantly, Ross reached out his hand. Jamie placed the coins in it, then stroked his hand with her finger as she drew it away. Then she and her friend laughed as she took the gum and they left. Donnelly, who had silently watched the entire exchange, then came back to the counter.

"Looks like somebody has their sights set on you," he teased.

"Her father, most likely…" Ross replied, "…with his hunting rifle."

Donnelly raised an eyebrow. "Even looking the way you do?"

"You have to understand, Agent Donnelly, that of all the people in this town, no one occupies as insecure a position as I. My Negro blood makes me an outcast among Whites, but my physical features make me untrusted by Blacks. My presence, my very appearance, disturbs them all on a deeply instinctive level, and in ways they don't understand. In short, I am a pariah of the worst sort – a leper among lepers."

"I can't imagine what it must be like for you. Why do you stay here then?"

Ross sighed. "I stay here because of a dilemma of self. Personal demons of an intense and powerful nature continually compel me to discard the path I currently walk upon in favor of another – one that is a road of shame, but that is growing in its power to move me because of the ease and luxury it provides."

Donnelly's brow furrowed in thought for a moment, then the truth dawned upon him.

"You're considering crossing the color line," he concluded. "You're thinking of passing for White."

Chapter 35

Ross didn't immediately respond, then nodded his head shamefully.

"Passing," he said, uttering the word with an emotion that seemed to simultaneously comprise both contempt and longing. "It is a temptation that few men ever have to face. Why I must be one of them, I do not know."

Suddenly, the door opened and Mama Lu came in – *sans* alligator and holding a basket into which she began piling items off the shelves.

Donnelly, watching her from the corner of his eye, continued speaking.

"I could understand why you'd want to," he said. "No more sitting at the back of the bus, having to come into restaurants from the back, being refused service..."

"No, it's more than that," Ross insisted, then paused for a moment. "You know, a few years ago there was a Creole man named Daniel Lacour who was very fair, and somehow a plan to pass himself off as White crystallized in his mind. He moved to a new city where no one knew him, and began the charade. Believe it or not, it actually worked for a few years. But somehow, someway, word leaked out. Perhaps LaCour had one too many whiskey sours one night and let something slip, or maybe somebody he knew before recognized him. Either way, his secret soon became common knowledge. He was scared at first, but the Whites told him that he was their friend, and that they weren't going to harm a hair on his head."

"And then they killed him?" Donnelly presumed.

"No," Ross answered, shaking his head. "They were true to their word. They didn't hurt him at all. What they did do, however, was tie him down in the middle of the swamp, pour pig blood over him, and leave him there. How long do you think it was before every creature in the swamp smelled that blood and came along to get a piece of that man for dinner?"

Donnelly didn't verbally respond, but the shock and horror on his face said volumes.

"As you can tell," Ross continued, "passing is not a game that you can simply quit when you start losing. It's all or nothing, win or die. You have to have a trump card or a secret weapon…a foolproof plan of some sort for success in that kind of venture."

"I think I understand."

"I honestly doubt that you do, Agent Donnelly, but that is a discussion for another time," Ross declared. "Now, you were asking me about the mansion."

"That's right," Donnelly confirmed. "We think that Jaspar and Susie were staying there. Do you know anything about that?"

"No, I'm afraid I don't. I rarely checked on the house, and actually used it even less. It's entirely possible that they could have lived there undetected. It's located in an out-of-the way spot, and right on the edge of the swamp."

"Yeah, we noticed that," Donnelly told him.

At that moment, Mama Lu – carrying a full basket now – exited the store, muttering to herself. Donnelly watched her leave, then noted her standing outside the store window, holding the basket and talking loudly to what he assumed was an imaginary friend.

"Do you let just anyone come in here and waltz out like that without paying?" he asked.

"No," Ross stated, "but Mama Lu's special."

"You can say that again."

Ross frowned. "She wasn't always how she is now: old and senile. I'm told that at one time she was a very beautiful woman. No one knows where she came from...she just came marching up out of the swamp one day carrying her baby girl with her. Rumor says that the folks in her hometown felt she was too beautiful for a Black man, so they killed her husband, but she managed to escape. They say she walked over two hundred miles, carrying her child the entire way, until she got here."

"That's incredible," Donnelly remarked, plainly impressed.

"Agreed, but her troubles didn't end there. A few years later, the same problem arose again. A White man wanted her and felt he should be able to take her if he so desired, so he tried."

"What happened?"

"She killed him for his efforts – stabbed him to death. Of course the whole town was in an uproar. Never mind the fact that this man had attempted to rape a woman, a nigger had killed a White person. That's all that mattered. I can only imagine what would have happened had they caught her, but they never did. She vanished into the swamp."

Donnelly glanced out the window at Mama Lu again, still standing outside.

"Since they couldn't hurt *her*," Ross continued, "they hurt her by proxy. They took her fifteen year-old daughter and had their way with her. Seventeen men...all of them. The girl's mind snapped."

"She was never right after that," Ross went on. "Even worse, months after the event, it was discovered that she was pregnant. Ultimately, she bore twin girls. One of them was Jaspar's mother; the other was mine."

Now at a loss for words, Donnelly simply muttered, "I'm sorry…"

Ross shrugged. "It's not of any consequence anymore."

"But you really are more White than Black," Donnelly observed.

"Are you surprised by that? That race-mixing occurs, despite how many Whites feel about Blacks? Apparently, miscegenation is a concept abhorred in word, but practiced in deed."

"And you say they never caught her?" Donnelly inquired, tilting his head towards Mama Lu.

"No," Ross replied. "And when she did finally reappear, no one went after her. Given what had happened to her daughter, everyone seemingly felt that justice had been served. Unsurprisingly, she never moved back to Evangeline proper…other than occasional forays into town, she just stayed out in the swamp."

Donnelly didn't say anything, but he now understood why Ross seemed to have a soft spot for Mama Lu.

"So tell me," Ross blurted out, changing the subject, "did you find anything at the mansion?"

Donnelly nodded and then, almost reluctantly, handed him the bag he was still holding, saying, "Yeah, we found this."

Without hesitation, Ross reached into the paper sack and pulled out a clear plastic bag. Inside it were the skeletal remains of a right hand. Ross simply stared at it in silence for a moment.

"Jaspar's?" he finally asked after a few seconds.

"We think so," Donnelly acknowledged.

"The sheriff's a hard man, but until this moment I never really thought him capable of this. I can only imagine what he did to poor Susie."

Donnelly gave him a curious look. "You don't think he'd kill his own daughter, do you?"

"Why not?" Ross demanded. "He killed his own son…"

Chapter 36

Agent Kimble cracked open the door to the schoolhouse and peeked inside. Ginger Meadows was at the front of the class going over a math problem. He had tried to be inconspicuous, but she noticed him almost immediately. At that juncture, he motioned for her to come to him.

Ginger gave him a subtle nod and then stated, "Class, you'll have to excuse me for a moment. Hattie Mae, please take over."

Hattie Mae glanced sheepishly at Kimble, then lowered her head and ambled towards the front of the class as Ginger walked towards the FBI agent. A moment later, the two of them stepped from the room.

"It's nice to see you again, Ginger," Kimble told her with a smile.

"Same here, Agent Kimble," she responded in a flat tone.

"Hmmm," he droned. "I noticed you asked that same girl – Hattie Mae – to take lead again when you stepped away to talk to me."

"Yes," Ginger stated with a nod. "She's bright, eager to learn, and is great with the other students. In my opinion, she'd make a fantastic teacher – if she can ever get out of this town."

"Seems like a lot of responsibility to put on a young girl. How old is she, by the way?"

"Seventeen," she replied. "But I'm sure you're not here to ask me about my students, Agent Kimble."

"It's Billy," he asserted. "I go by Billy."

She gave him an odd look. "Isn't that a bit familiar – getting on a first-name basis with people involved in your investigation?"

Her words were ironically similar to what his partner had said previously, but Kimble merely shrugged. "It depends. Sometimes it's helpful if you're trying to build rapport with someone. Plus, you're a witness, not a suspect."

"Still, it's more informal than I expected from a federal agent."

"Well, to be honest, it's how I prefer to be addressed. I was *Billy* Kimble long before I was *Agent* Kimble, and I just feel it suits me better."

"Billy, then," she said. "How can I help you?"

"We're still trying to get a handle on this Susie-Jaspar thing. You see, we know that they were living out at the old Michaels place. We also know that Susie was pregnant."

"Pregnant?" Ginger repeated. "What makes you say that?"

Kimble didn't reply. Instead, he walked over to the door leading outside and opened it. He then reached out and pulled the charred remains of a baby crib into the vestibule. Ginger covered her mouth with her hand when she saw it, stifling a gasp. Moments later, her eyes began to water.

"Oh, no!" she muttered. "No! No! No!"

Holding the crib in front of him, Kimble said, "We found this in the remains of the mansion. It was obviously old, but it looks like somebody went through some trouble to fix it up."

Trembling, Ginger reached out and touched the crib lightly, almost as if she couldn't believe it was real.

"You knew, didn't you?" Kimble prodded. "You knew Susie was pregnant."

Ginger nodded, then began weeping softly. Kimble swiftly handed her his handkerchief.

"Y-y-yes," she managed to say between sobs. "Susie t-t-told me before they l-l-left."

"Did you know where they were staying?" Kimble inquired.

"I wasn't sure," Ginger told him, at the same time wiping her eyes with the handkerchief. "Ross didn't tell me anything; he said it was better if I didn't know...safer for me."

"So Ross knew?"

"I think so," Ginger told him. "They're dead aren't they? Not just Jaspar, but Susie and the baby, too!"

"Hush now," Kimble insisted, putting his arms around her and pulling her in close in a comforting – but platonic – hug. "We don't know that."

"But where else could they be?" she practically demanded. "They can't be anywhere *but* dead."

Chapter 37

Kimble didn't immediately respond to Ginger's statement, choosing instead to keep his arms around her – offering sympathetic comfort for a moment until she stepped back a few seconds later.

Drying her eyes one last time, Ginger handed the handkerchief back to Kimble, saying, "There. I think I'm all done."

"So am I," he told her, plainly indicating that he didn't have any more questions.

"Well, I suppose I should get back to my class now. Nice to see you again, Billy."

With that she turned to go back in, but stopped and spun around at the sound of his voice.

"Mind if I ask you an unrelated question?" he inquired.

She shrugged. "Sure."

Kimble made a sweeping motion with his hand that encompassed the entire school. "Why do you do all this?"

Ginger chuckled slightly as she walked back towards him. She crossed her arms and leaned against the wall.

"The school, you mean? Because I enjoy teaching," she told him.

"No, I mean why *here*? Why at an all-Black school instead of one that's all White, or even a place that's integrated?"

"At one time I did. I taught at an integrated school, and I thought I was a pretty good teacher. I treated all my students the same, or at least I believed I did."

"What changed that?"

"Believe it or not, something as simple as a spelling bee. In the finals of the third grade competition, it came down to a battle between a little Black girl and a little White boy, both of whom were my students. To make a long story short, the Black girl – Emily was her name – won. But because the school didn't want to have a Black champion, and because some people couldn't stomach the thought of a Black child being smarter than a White one, she gave a correct answer that the judges marked as wrong."

"I'm not saying it's right," Kimble noted, "but that doesn't seem like such a big deal."

"There's more. Emily's father was absolutely furious, and he came to me because she was my student. He said that he was taking her out of my class, because he knew that Whites hated all Blacks, but he thought we could show a little tolerance. I became furious myself and shouted that I didn't hate Blacks, that I'd never done anything to hurt a Negro. Then he said something that struck me to the core."

"Which was what?"

Ginger paused for a moment, obviously reflecting on what had happened. "He said that it wasn't enough just to not do anything to hurt them. If I wasn't actively supporting Negro advancement, then I was actively working against them, and he was right."

"How's that?" Kimble asked with a frown.

"There's an old saying: All that's necessary for evil to triumph is for good men to do nothing."

"I've heard it."

"Well, it holds true in terms of racial issues. By doing nothing, you're saying that you are comfortable with the status quo and the racist system we currently live under," she replied. "Unless you actively seek to make a change for the better, then you are part of the problem, not the solution, and your actions – or inactions, rather – help perpetuate the current system."

"Basically," she continued, "we Whites can't just continue to pat ourselves on the back and feel good about ourselves just because we personally haven't harmed any Blacks. We have to proactively advocate for change, so this is the way I choose to fight...I'm here in a place where I make a difference."

"So you're saying that no one's neutral – that by action or inaction, everyone is either working for or against racial equality," Kimble concluded. "Seems kind of absolutist."

"There's no middle ground here, Billy. You're either on one side of the fence or the other," she insisted. "It's as simple as black and white."

Ginger then walked back into the classroom, leaving Kimble to ponder her words.

Chapter 38

Ross was sweeping the store with his back to the door when he heard someone enter.

He shouted over his shoulder without turning around, stating, "We're closed. You'll have to come back tomorrow."

The harsh voice of the sheriff responded, declaring, "Well, you gonna stay open a little late tonight, boy."

Ross turned to see Sheriff Washburn, his deputy, and a few other men standing at the front of the store. From the dour expressions on their faces, it was clear that this wasn't a friendly visit in any way, manner, or form. Nevertheless, Ross leaned his broom against a nearby wall and casually approached them, stopping a few feet away.

"I'm happy to extend our store hours in this instance," he said politely. "How can I help you gentlemen?"

"Gentlemen?" the sheriff echoed mockingly, causing the others with him to chortle. "Hell boy, gentlemen's the last thing we are, but I like that! It shows the proper level of respect."

Ross merely stood his ground as Washburn then came over and put an arm around his shoulders in a congenial fashion. At the same time, Conners lowered the blinds on the store's main window while one of the other men locked the door. Meanwhile, the sheriff began maneuvering Ross towards the group accompanying him.

"Now then, down to business," Sheriff Washburn said. "Ross, I was under the impression that you and I had an understanding about this business concerning your cousin. That's why it hurts and confuses me when I see things like you spending so much time with the G-men, just chatting it up with'em in front of your store window like you were a lil' while ago. Do you wanna know how much it hurts me? *This* much!"

He suddenly landed a powerful punch to Ross's stomach. Ross felt all of the air rush forcefully from his body and he crumbled to the floor, holding his stomach and retching violently.

"I feel…" Ross mumbled, struggling for breath. "I feel… I feel your pain."

Washburn chuckled unexpectedly, as did the other men with him.

"I'll be damned," the sheriff uttered. "Looks like we got a comedian here, fellas."

While his compatriots continued laughing, Washburn suddenly glared at Ross, saying, "You wanna know what *I* find funny? I mean absolutely, side-splitting, knee-slapping hilarious? *This*!"

As he finished speaking, he lashed out with a boot, catching Ross in the side with a kick so hard that it flipped him over.

"And *this*!" the sheriff added, kicking him again. "And *this*!"

Ross lay on the floor, moaning and wincing in agony as Sheriff Washburn took a step back, apparently taking a breather.

"So that's *my* comedy act," Washburn grumbled, while those with him continued chuckling. "You find it funny, Mr. Comedian?"

"No…" Ross groaned, shaking his head while still grimacing in pain. "I don't like improv…"

The sheriff and the others all looked at each other, plainly befuddled by Ross's comment. Noting their confusion, Ross suddenly burst out laughing, despite the pain it caused in places where he'd been kicked and punched. In his mind, however, it was worth the tradeoff.

"Dammit, Zeke!" Deputy Conners blurted out angrily. "This albino nigger's making fun of us!"

"He won't be laughing for long," Washburn promised. "Get him up."

Several of the men stepped forward and roughly hauled Ross to his feet. A moment later, Conners put a knife to his throat.

"Listen close," the deputy practically hissed. "You got one chance, nigger, just one, of coming out of this alive - and maybe in one piece. Now, you tell us everything you told those FBI guys, and I mean *everything*!"

Chapter 39

Donnelly was sitting on his bed in their hotel room when his partner came in. Kimble took off his coat and tossed it across a chair, then stretched out on his own bed.

"So," Donnelly droned, "did you get anything?"

"Yeah," Kimble replied. "First and foremost, the girl we saw at Reverend Bridge's place is seventeen, according to Ginger."

"Which means she's at the age of consent."

"Right," Kimble affirmed. "So even if what you suspect about her and the good reverend is true, there's nothing to be done. His behavior might be despicable, but it isn't criminal."

"So it would seem," Donnelly noted with a sour look. "Anything else?"

"Apparently Ginger knew Susie was pregnant...also had an idea of where they might have been staying. But she said Ross probably knew for sure."

"That's funny. Ross said he didn't have a clue."

"Hmmm," Kimble mused. "Food for thought…"

"There's more, though," Donnelly added.

"Oh?" Kimble muttered. "What, pray tell?"

"The sheriff – he was Jaspar's father."

"What?!" Kimble exclaimed, bolting upright.

Donnelly had his notepad out and was perusing it closely.

"Apparently it's common knowledge here," he explained. "And according to Ross, it's one of the reasons Jaspar was so eager to work at the sheriff's place."

"He wanted to be part of the family," Kimble concluded.

"Exactly," Donnelly confirmed, nodding. "Except he jumped from trying to be *part* of the family to *starting* one. He got his own sister, half-sister anyway, pregnant. Can you believe it?"

Kimble shrugged. "These things happen."

"Shit, Billy!" Donnelly blurted out. "You make it sound like this happens every day."

"Actually, it does."

"I thought that was just a stereotype – that there's lots of incest in the South."

"I don't know how to quantify 'lots' in this instance," Kimble told him, "but it does happen, and not just in the South. Incest happens all over, so I'm not stunned when I come across it on occasion. And Black and White mixing doesn't shock me either. I'm shocked at the fact that it's the sheriff, though. He strikes me as a true nigger-hater."

"We're on the same page there," his partner stated.

Leaning over, Kimble took the notepad from Donnelly.

"What else does it say?" he asked as he began flipping through the pages.

"Not much...just a few other things Ross said, like about being a pariah."

"You mean he thinks he's a fish?" Kimble asked.

"No, not a *piranha*," Donnelly corrected. "A *pariah*. It means he's…"

He trailed off as he suddenly noticed his partner grinning at him.

"You're yanking my chain," Donnelly surmised. "You know what a pariah is."

"An outcast, maybe?" Kimble offered, still smiling.

"Anyway," Donnelly continued, "the only other things are my conclusions – that Susie and Jaspar ran off together after she found out she was pregnant. And that the Sheriff killed Jaspar…and probably Susie and the baby as well. Zeke Washburn's heart must be black, to kill his own children like that."

"You obviously don't understand how deep racial prejudice runs," Kimble admonished. "I'm from the South, and I've known plenty of men who flat-out would rather kill their sisters and daughters than see them with Black men."

"Washburn's apparently one of those. And it probably didn't help that – unlike Ross – Jaspar actually looked Black, despite his mixed heritage. Still it's hard to believe that even the sheriff is capable of what we're talking about."

"Then tell me," Kimble said. "What would *you* do if your Black son got your White daughter pregnant? Hmmm?"

Donnelly frowned, plainly reflecting on the question, but didn't answer.

"Anyway," Kimble continued, "I suggest we confront the sheriff about all this tomorrow, although this damn town is likely to explode when we do. With that in mind, I'm going to take a shower and try to get one last good night of sleep. I suggest you do the same."

"You practically read my mind," Donnelly stated in reply.

Chapter 40

It was late when Agent Kimble opened his eyes, then spent a moment watching his snoozing partner, who was currently covered by blankets and sheets. At the same time, he listened and heard deep, even breathing that he interpreted as heavy slumber. Now certain sure that Donnelly was sleeping soundly, Kimble got out of bed and quietly got dressed. He took a final look at Donnelly, then slipped out of the room.

As soon as Kimble left, Donnelly opened his eyes. Whipping back the covers, he jumped out of bed, already fully dressed. He quickly put on his shoes and hastily – but quietly – exited the room.

Going downstairs, Donnelly dashed to a window and peeked out. The night was dark, but by the light of a streetlamp he saw Kimble get into a truck being driven by Deputy Conners. As the truck pulled away, Donnelly raced outside and got into the agents' car. Leaving his lights out, he began following the truck.

****

It was a bit of a rough ride for Donnelly. Driving without lights meant failing to see a lot of bad road conditions: potholes, debris, etcetera. It also meant going a little slower than normal – especially on dirt roads that cut across the swamps. Still, thanks to their headlights, he managed to keep sight of the truck his partner was in, which ultimately came to a halt at the edge of an expansive cornfield.

Donnelly stopped and parked off the road near a group of trees. As he watched, the truck's headlights went out, but not before they allowed him to catch sight of numerous other vehicles nearby. A few seconds later, he spotted what appeared to be two flashlight beams – presumably his partner and the deputy. The two men then began making their way through the cornfield.

Although he had a flashlight of his own, Donnelly decided to keep it off as he hurried after the duo ahead of him. They didn't have much of a head start, and he felt confident he could trail them without being seen.

Unfortunately, the cornfield quickly obscured the illumination from the flashlights of Kimble and Conners. However, Donnelly did note the general direction in which they were heading. Therefore, facing that route, he tried jumping straight up into the air. His head didn't completely clear the cornstalks around him, but he caught a glimpse of a well-lit area ahead. Thus, after landing back on the ground, he tried going in a straight line in that direction.

About a minute later, he found himself approaching a clearing. Gliding quietly through the corn, he stopped just shy of the open area, staying hidden in the stalks while he scanned the space in front of him.

In the middle of the clearing a hefty cross was burning, illuminating much of the area. In addition, a large number of men were standing around in white sheets and hoods: Klansmen.

In the middle of everything, Donnelly spotted the sheriff, with his hood back and wearing the emblem of the Grand Dragon. Next to him was a still-hooded man, and the two of them laughed and joked with each other for a moment. In fact, most of those present appeared to be engaged in animated conversation, filling the air with chatter. Donnelly clenched his teeth as he scoured the crowd, looking for his partner.

"Okay, Billy," he muttered to himself. "Where are you…?"

Suddenly, the sheriff raised his hands for silence.

"Settle down everybody," Washburn belted out. "I said, settle down!"

Almost immediately, all conversation came to an abrupt halt.

"That's better," Washburn continued. "Now, I want y'all to meet an associate." He then gestured towards the Klansman next to him. "He's new to these parts, but not new to the Klan, and has been a full-fledged member for almost twenty years. He's only gonna be here for a few more days, so let's make sure we show him a good time."

All of the gathered Klansmen began cheering loudly, as if to verbally express their hospitality. Sheriff Washburn leaned towards the man beside him and said something that Donnelly was clearly too far away to catch, but he saw the other man give a curt nod in response.

"Alright, alright," the sheriff bellowed, causing everyone to quiet down again. "Our newest member has a few words to say."

At that moment, the man Sheriff Washburn had been joking with pulled back his hood.

It was Agent Kimble.

Chapter 41

Donnelly was so shocked that his mouth almost fell open.

You bastard! he thought as he watched his partner standing there proudly in Klan regalia. It was all Donnelly could do not to run out and sock him in the mouth.

Now the center of attention, Kimble simply looked around for a moment at those assembled, who were clearly waiting for him to speak.

"Well," Kimble began, "I think I met most of you the other night–"

"And wasn't that some fun?" Conners interjected, causing several of those present to guffaw and cheer.

Luthor… Donnelly said to himself, mentally identifying what he felt Conners was referring to.

"Anyway," Kimble continued, "most of you know why I'm here, but I just want you to know that you ain't got nothing to worry about." At that point, he patted Washburn congenially on the shoulder, then said, "The sheriff and me, we think alike on a lot of things – one of those being that he's got everything here under control. So you have my word that my dumbass partner and I will be on our way in a day or two and leave you good people in peace."

The Klansmen made general murmurs of agreement with this, expressing their satisfaction with his statement.

"Don't worry," Sheriff Washburn told Kimble, while speaking loud enough for everyone to hear. "We've got a plan that'll keep your partner out of any more trouble."

Deputy Conners and several other Klansmen laughed wildly at this, while Kimble looked a little unsure. Back in his hiding place, Donnelly angrily snapped a cornstalk, but thankfully the noise went unheard. Feeling he'd seen enough, Donnelly crept stealthily back to the car.

****

Kimble was trying to sneak quietly into the hotel room when the lights suddenly came on. Donnelly, fully dressed, was sitting in a chair with his gun pointed at his partner. Kimble slowly raised his hands.

"Now take it easy, kid," Kimble advised. "Don't do anything rash."

"Rash?" Donnelly repeated, his fury evident. "You mean like sell out my partner in favor of the Klan?"

"You followed me!" Kimble exclaimed with a smile. "I have to tell you, I'm really surprised. You're a better agent than I gave you credit for."

"Save the compliments for the judge. Now put these on."

As he finished speaking, Donnelly tossed a pair of handcuffs at his partner, who caught them.

"Kid…" Kimble began. "I mean, Trevor – let me explain. It's the old saying: keep your friends close, but your enemies closer. What you saw tonight was me trying to get some inside information."

Scowling, Donnelly leaped to his feet. "I'm just one step from blowing your fucking head off! Now shut up and put the cuffs on!"

Kimble stared at the handcuffs for a moment. However, before he could do anything else, the phone rang.

The two agents just looked at each other. It was the first time the phone had rang since they'd arrived, and it was far too late for casual conversation. As they both contemplated who it could be, the phone rang again.

"Want me to get that?" Kimble finally asked.

Donnelly considered for a moment, then said, "Go ahead."

Kimble walked over to the phone and picked it up. Donnelly, still holding the gun, stepped towards him and made him hold the receiver away from his ear so they both could hear.

"Hello?" said Kimble.

"Is your partner there?" said a voice that both agents recognized as Deputy Conners.

Kimble looked at Donnelly, who nodded.

"Yeah," Kimble replied. "He's here."

"Tell him to take a peek out the window."

Although he knew Donnelly had heard the message, Kimble stated, "He says to look out the window."

Still keeping his gun on Kimble, Donnelly walked to the window. Angling himself so that he could still see his partner with his peripheral vision (and take action if he tried anything), Donnelly risked taking a glance outside.

"I don't see anything," he declared.

"Now," said Conners, "tell him I said…goodbye!"

Just then, Donnelly saw light glinting off metal on a nearby roof. A moment later, the sound of a gun going off boomed like a cannon, as buckshot ripped through the window of the agents' room.

Chapter 42

Diving haphazardly to the side, Donnelly just barely managed to avoid getting shredded by buckshot. The pellets shattered the window, sending glass shards flying through the room. That said, the drapes somehow managed to stay attached to the curtain rod; although now tattered, they would make it difficult for the shooter to get a clear shot at anyone in the room. (And Donnelly had no intention of making himself an easy target by peeking out again.)

Although flinging himself away from the window had clearly saved his life, the process of doing so caused Donnelly to lose his grip on his gun. In short, as he went down, it went sliding to the other side of the room.

He swiftly came to his feet, preparing to go retrieve it. However, he'd barely taken a step before a heavy hand fell unexpectedly on his shoulder and spun him around.

It was his partner, of course. It looked as though Kimble were about to say something, but Donnelly never gave him a chance. Without preamble, he threw a punch that landed squarely on Kimble's jaw, sending him staggering back into the wall.

As Donnelly came at him again, Kimble kicked him in the shin. Donnelly yelped and began hopping around on one foot. Kimble stepped towards him, pulling back his arm as if to sock his partner in the face, but Donnelly suddenly landed a punch to Kimble's stomach, doubling him over.

Now standing on both feet, Donnelly locked his fingers together and smashed down on the center of his partner's back; Kimble crashed to the floor. At that point, Donnelly kicked him in the side. However, when he tried to kick him a second time. Kimble caught the offending foot.

Kimble twisted the foot he held and Donnelly went down to the floor. Before he could move, Kimble was on top of him and struck him solidly on the jaw two times. He is about to hit him again when he noticed that Donnelly was already half-dazed.

Getting off his partner, Kimble then picked up Donnelly's gun from the floor. Next, he retrieved his own firearm off the dresser as Donnelly slowly rose to his feet.

Donnelly looked at the guns that Kimble held. "Now what?"

"Now we–" Kimble began, but stopped abruptly and turned as the door to their room burst open and Deputy Conners ran in, followed by three other men, all with guns.

"Hands up!" the deputy yelled, as he and those with him aimed their weapons at the two agents.

With Donnelly now standing slightly behind him and to one side, Kimble raised his hands as high as they would go. The movement lifted up his jacket, revealing the gun he kept tucked at his back to Donnelly.

"Whoa there!" Kimble blurted out. "Whoa! Don't shoot! I'm on your side, remember? Can I put my hands down?"

Conners grinned sheepishly at that. Meanwhile, Donnelly eyed the gun at his partner's back, weighing his chances.

"Sure, go ahead," the deputy answered a few seconds later.

All of a sudden, Ms. Broussard – in a nightgown, rollers, and nightmask – stuck her head in the door.

"What the hell is going on in here?" she demanded. "You can't just come in here tearing up my place like this!"

"Official business, you old goat," Conners told her. "Go back to bed."

"And you go to hell!" Ms. Broussard shot back. "Tell Zeke he'll be getting a bill from me!"

She then stormed off in a huff. While everyone's attention was still centered on her, Donnelly quickly stepped forward and yanked the gun out of his partner's pants. Kimble immediately dove to the floor as Donnelly began firing.

Donnelly took out one of his assailants with a bullet to the head at point-blank range. He shot a second in the chest and the man went down, although Donnelly couldn't immediately tell he was alive or dead.

At that point, Deputy Conners was already dashing from the room, firing blindly behind him. Most of his shots went wild, but one struck his third compatriot in the back, and the man dropped to the floor, wailing in pain.

That left the two FBI agents as the only able-bodied people left in the room. However, before Kimble could rise from the floor, Donnelly clubbed him on the back of the head with the gun, knocking him out. Fighting the temptation to shoot his unconscious partner, Donnelly settled for retrieving his own weapon and then ran from the room.

Chapter 43

After leaving the hotel room, Donnelly was wary of running into another ambush. However, Conners had seemingly only brought the three others who had been with him, and the deputy himself had apparently fled the premises when the gunplay broke out. Still, Donnelly had remained cautious and exited the hotel by slipping out a side window and then stuck to the shadows as he crept away.

It turned out to be the right decision, as he soon saw several sets of flashlights on the streets. One of them was quite likely the rooftop shooter who had tried to blast him (and possibly intent on finishing the job).

The shooter obviously couldn't have been Deputy Conners – he and his trio had gotten to the agents' hotel room way too quickly. Plus, the deputy had actually been on the phone when the shooting occurred. Taken altogether, the facts suggested that Conners had called their room from inside the hotel and simply signaled the shooter in some fashion.

Donnelly didn't kid himself; he had gotten lucky – twice – in the hotel room. But, even keeping to the shadows, his luck wouldn't hold out for long with the sheriff's cronies out patrolling the area. And if they weren't looking for him already they soon would be, which indicated one course of action: he needed to get off the street.

That was easier said than done. He really didn't have any friends in Evangeline. Even worse, his own partner had turned out to be in league with the enemy. His best option was to get the hell out of this town. Barring that, he needed to find a place to hunker down. However, the only people who might open their door to him were Ginger Meadows and Ross Johnson, and between them, Ross – who lived above the store he ran – was undoubtedly the closest.

That said, Donnelly decided to at least make an effort to get to the car, even though there was bound to be someone keeping an eye on it. Much to his surprise, however, the vehicle turned out to be unguarded. Not believing his luck, he stealthily approached the driver's side, preparing to jump in and drive off. He would be leaving some things unresolved, but there was still some evidence in the trunk. It wasn't much, but it would hopefully be enough to at least bring charges.

And it was then, as he reflected on the evidence and what it signified, that an entirely new line of thought suddenly occurred to him…

****

Ross was sleeping soundly in his bed when the light suddenly came on. The harsh, unexpected brightness made him wince as he abruptly came awake. It was at that point that he realized there was a gun pointed at his head.

"Agent Donnelly," Ross muttered as he saw who was holding the weapon. "Nice to see you again."

Donnelly slowly stepped back as Ross rose to a sitting position. Grabbing a pair of pants laying across a nearby chair, he tossed them to Ross.

"Get dressed," Donnelly ordered.

Ross got out of bed and began putting the pants on, pulling them up over some briefs he had been sleeping in.

"May I ask what this is about?" Ross inquired.

"Sure," Donnelly replied. "It's about you being arrested for being a conspirator in three murders."

"No," Ross told him. "You're mistaken."

"Oh, am I? Then why does everything in this case keep coming back to you?" Donnelly demanded. "Who knew that Susie was pregnant? You. Who owned the house where she and Jaspar stayed? You. Who knew they were there? You. It all comes back to *you*."

Ross remained calm as he continued dressing. "So what gave it away?"

"This," Donnelly answered as he reached into his pocket and pulled out a charred rag, but with some legible writing still on it that spelled a single word: FLOUR.

"That's the same kind of flour bag you used to give meat to little Bobby," Donnelly continued. "We found it in the rubble of the Michaels mansion. So I'm guessing you brought Susie and Jaspar food, which means you knew where they were. In fact, you were the *only* one who knew, so it had to be you that ratted them out."

Donnelly spoke with conviction, but in truth, his statements conveyed a conclusion he had only reached minutes earlier – when he was preparing to get in the car and leave town as fast as humanly possible. Maybe it was the adrenaline, but in thinking about the evidence they had collected and the facts, he had unexpectedly realized that some of it could point in a very different direction than what he had initially assumed. Thus, rather than skedaddle, he had retrieved the charred "FLOUR" rag from the trunk and set off for Ross's place. Once there, he was unsurprised to find that Ross followed the common practice of not locking his door.

Now, as he watched Ross finish dressing, Donnelly pressed for answers, saying, "What kind of deal did they offer you, huh? What kind of promises did they make to get you to sell out your own cousin? What did they do, Ross, offer to let you pass for White? Was that it?"

"And what if it was?" Ross asked defiantly.

"You sick bastard," Donnelly hissed. "I ought to blast you where you stand, but I need you to convict the others. Come on."

As he finished speaking, Donnelly motioned Ross towards the door with the gun.

"Where are we going?" inquired Ross.

"To my car," Donnelly told him. "Then we're getting the hell out of this town and you're going to testify."

"And if I refuse?"

"Then I shoot you right now."

Ross simply nodded. "Fair enough."

He then opened the door and stepped out, followed by Donnelly. They were now on a narrow set of stairs behind the store that led up to Ross's room. Suddenly, the voice of Deputy Conners cut through the darkness.

"There they are!" Conners yelled. "Get'em!"

Chapter 44

Bullets bit into the wood and brick around them as Ross dove headlong down the stairs and Donnelly hurled himself over the railing.

Donnelly landed in a crouch; Ross rolled to the bottom of the stairs then spun around underneath them, where Donnelly was already waiting. With gunfire still ringing around them, Ross moved into a sprint position, obviously in preparation to run. That's when he felt Donnelly's gun at the back of his head.

"Where do you think you're going, asshole?" Donnelly blurted out.

"We can't stay here!" Ross stressed forcefully. "They'll have us pinned down in a minute. We have to run for it."

Donnelly deliberated for a moment. In the meantime, Ross cringed as a bullet caromed off the brick wall next to him.

"Alright," Donnelly conceded. "We'll head to my car, so go where I tell you. And if you make one move in any other direction, I'll shoot you in the back."

Ross nodded, then dashed out. Hot on his heels was Donnelly, who fired in the direction of their assailants in an effort to provide cover.

****

Somehow, they managed to reach the car unscathed, albeit out of breath, just as dawn was starting to break.

"Drive!" Donnelly commanded, tossing the keys to Ross as they drew near the vehicle.

A second later, they were inside the car. Not far away, several men with guns suddenly came rushing out into the street.

Ross started the car, and with a squeal of burning rubber went zooming down the avenue. Donnelly, with his gun still pointed at Ross, split his attention between watching his prisoner and watching the road. The men with guns scattered as the car came racing towards them, barely managing to avoid getting hit. Ross then made a skillful turn, putting them on the road heading out of town.

They rode in tense silence for a minute or so, then Ross let out a deep breath in obvious relief.

"I think we're clear now," he stated. "You can put the gun away."

"Gee, thanks for the offer," Donnelly replied, "but seeing that I hold you responsible for the deaths of three people, I'd like to keep you in custody."

"No, you don't understand," Ross began explaining. "I – oh shit!"

Looking out the windshield ahead of them, Donnelly saw what had caused Ross's outburst. They had just come around a tree-lined curve, and there – parked across the thoroughfare and effectively serving as a roadblock – was the sheriff's car.

Donnelly caught a brief glimpse of Sheriff Washburn's face, sporting a smug expression as he stood near the front of the car. He also noted another person nearby: his partner, Agent Kimble.

At that juncture, Ross went veering off the road, plainly attempting to avoid a collision and prompting Donnelly to shout "Look out!"

They swerved wildly – making Washburn and Kimble dive for safety in the process – but managed to skirt the sheriff's vehicle without making contact. However, in attempting to get the car back on the road, Ross apparently lost control. The car fishtailed for a moment, then went spinning to the side before unexpectedly flying off the roadway. It then went flipping end-over-end like a tumbleweed before ultimately coming to rest on its roof far from the road.

Donnelly, shaken and more than a little dazed, took a moment to look around and get his bearings. Wearing his seatbelt had probably saved his life, and as he released it and collapsed to the roof of the car, he immediately noticed two things.

First, there was no one in the driver's seat. The driver's side door was open, and – looking in that direction – he noticed Ross limping into the cover of the misty swamp.

The other thing that made an impression on him was the sheriff's car. Or rather, the fact that it was headed in his direction, presumably with his partner and Washburn inside.

Crawling from the wreckage, Donnelly now had an idea of why the agents' car had been unguarded. With the road blocked, the sheriff had seemingly felt it was unnecessary. Sadly, he had been right.

But you bastards haven't caught me yet, Donnelly thought as he staggered into the swamp after Ross.

Chapter 45

Sheriff Washburn and Agent Kimble arrived just in time to see Donnelly disappearing into the mist of the swamp. Behind them, a truck full of men and dogs pulled up, with the hounds yapping loudly.

Kimble pointed with his chin towards the direction Donnelly had headed. "What's your opinion?"

Sheriff Washburn rubbed his chin in thought for a moment. "Normally, if one of you city boys goes into the swamp, you're not coming out – at least not upright. But he's got Ross with'im, and that's one smart rascal. We'd better go in after 'em."

With that, the two men opened their respective doors and stepped out. Kimble then made his way to the other side of the car, stopping just a few feet from the sheriff. At the same time, the men in the truck clambered out, all of them carrying firearms. Bringing the dogs with them, they headed towards the sheriff and Agent Kimble.

"Alright boys," Washburn began after the men had gathered round. "We got two of'em down there. Bring'em back alive if you can, and if you can't…well, dead might even be better!"

Everyone laughed, then the men and dogs began heading towards the swamp.

****

Donnelly focused on trying to travel in a straight line, continuing in the direction he'd seen Ross headed. With the mist hindering his vision, however, it was more than a little difficult. In addition, he found himself continually distracted by the sounds of the swamp – weird chirps, drones, and growls (among other things) coming from all around him. Even worse, many of the noises were seemingly made by animals and insects that he was completely unfamiliar with.

All of a sudden, he heard the baying of hounds to his rear.

Shit! he thought to himself. *They've got dogs!*

He started running then. Fortunately, the morning sun was starting to burn off some of the mist, giving him a bit more visibility.

After a few minutes, he found himself at the edge of a small pond. Donnelly then came to an abrupt halt when he noticed that the pond wasn't exactly empty: in the middle of it was a large alligator.

Common sense told Donnelly that the wisest course of action was to circle around the water. However, the sound of dogs barking to his rear made him glance behind. He couldn't see his pursuers yet, but based on what he could hear of the hounds, they were getting closer. Ergo, at that moment, common sense went out the window.

Donnelly wasn't sure, but it looked like the gator was asleep. Moreover, the pond looked rather shallow – maybe knee-deep at worst. Decision made, he raced across the water.

Much to his chagrin, it turned out that the alligator actually wasn't asleep. Our perhaps his splashing across its habitat (or the baying of the dogs) disturbed its slumber. Regardless, as Donnelly dashed by, it snapped at him.

Thankfully, he had given the reptile a wide berth so that he was never in any real danger. However, that didn't make the incident any less alarming. Thus, upon reaching the other side of the pond, he only took a brief moment to glance behind him to ensure that the gator hadn't given chase (it hadn't), then continued on without breaking stride.

Behind him, Donnelly heard the sharp barking of the dogs suddenly shift to whining. He couldn't have sworn to it, but he was certain that meant his pursuers had come to the pond with the gator. That would buy him a little time, assuming they had to circle around and then give the dogs a minute or so to pick up his scent again.

Those thoughts and more were flitting through Donnelly's brain when, running hard and out of breath, he suddenly felt his feet go out from under him. At first, he thought he'd fallen into a pond, but he suddenly realized that he wasn't in water at all, but something else entirely.

Quicksand! he bellowed mentally. And he was in it up to his waist.

Moving ever so slowly (and trying not to panic), he reached out a hand for the solid ground that was nearby. He stretched as far as he could, but it was still a few inches beyond his reach.

Donnelly relaxed for a moment. Much to his surprise, he wasn't sinking any deeper. But that was the only good news, as he could once again hear the dogs and men behind him getting closer. Even if he didn't drown in the quicksand, being stuck there when Washburn and the others showed up would surely be just as bad (if not worse). With that thought to spur him on, he reached for solid ground again.

Come on..., he told him himself as he leaned out. *Just a little bit more...*

This time his fingers actually grazed the ground, but couldn't find purchase. Anxiously, he tried again and managed to grasp something akin to a tree root. For a moment, it looked as though it was anchored well enough for Donnelly to use it to draw himself out – and then it broke off in his hand.

Donnelly flung the root away in disgust. Now desperate, he stretched his hand out again for solid ground. This time, there was nothing within reach, and he found himself on the verge of despair. That's when a strong right hand suddenly reached down and gripped his.

Chapter 46

Agent Kimble, Sheriff Washburn and several other men were standing about fifty feet from the pond. The dogs, held on leashes by the remainder of the sheriff's party, were near the edge of the water. The hounds whined miserably while shambling back and forth, although a few of them occasionally barked at the nearby alligator in the pond, which hissed back at them.

"What's wrong with them dogs?" Washburn asked no one in particular. "They lose the scent?"

"Not exactly," Deputy Conners responded. "But it looks like he lit out across that pond, and, uh..."

"And what?" the sheriff demanded as his deputy trailed off.

"Well, there's a gator in it," the deputy stated, gesturing in the direction of the reptile. "Got the dogs spooked."

"Then kill the damn thing or go around it," Washburn growled. "We don't have all day, and this damn mist ain't makin' it any easier!"

"Goin' around's not a problem," the deputy assured him. "But from the way the dogs are actin', that gator's scent is all over the place. So even after we go around, it might take a minute or two to get them focused enough to pick up the trail again."

Washburn groaned in annoyance, then muttered, "Just do it."

****

Ross and Donnelly ran swiftly through the swamp. Behind them, they could hear the dogs and men coming after them. Donnelly wouldn't have sworn to it, but he guessed they were about five minutes ahead of those chasing them. If it came down to it, he still had his gun (which he had somehow managed to hang on to up to this point); however, it was covered in quicksand and probably not completely safe to fire.

All of a sudden, Ross came to a stop beneath a large tree with an odd bulbous flower growing on it.

"Wait a minute," Ross said, causing Donnelly to stop and double back for him.

"Look, I really appreciate you pulling me out the quicksand," Donnelly told him. "I probably would have drowned in it, so you saved my life. But I'll be throwing it away if I wait for those dogs to catch up to us."

As he finished speaking, Donnelly reflected on his rescue – how Ross had pulled him out of the bog. It wasn't something he suspected a guilty man would have done, and he'd quickly had to reevaluate (and dismiss) his perception of Ross as a suspect in his investigation.

"First of all," Ross remarked as he looked over the flower, "despite what the movies tell you, nobody drowns in quicksand. Any idiot around here can tell you that. You can get *stuck* in it, but you won't drown or go under."

Donnelly gave him a skeptical look. "Then why is it that I've read news reports of people dying in quicksand?"

"It's not the quicksand that kills them," Ross countered as he pulled two of the odd bulbs off the flower. "They get stuck in it and die of exposure, or it rains and the area floods so they drown that way, or something along those lines. But – as you probably realize from your own experience – they don't go under. The human body has too much buoyancy. At worst, you'll probably just sink down to your waist."

"So the only way to drown in quicksand is if you go in headfirst and get stuck."

"Pretty much," Ross confirmed with a nod as he sniffed the bulbs. "You're lucky that patch you fell in wasn't that viscous. Otherwise I wouldn't have been able to pull you out."

"Well again, I'm glad you did," Donnelly commented. "Even if I didn't go under, those dogs were right behind me."

Ross shook his head. "Actually, those mutts must have gotten held up or something, because they really weren't that close."

"Sure as hell sounded like it."

"That's the swamp," Ross told him. "It does weird things with acoustics, so things sometimes sound closer than they are. After a while, you develop an ear for it. But speaking of the dogs…"

As he trailed off, Ross crushed the two flower bulbs in his hands. A thick dark liquid began running out of them. He quickly began smearing it on himself – then unexpectedly began rubbing it on Donnelly's shirt as well.

"Holy shit!" Donnelly exclaimed, covering his nose. "What is that *smell*?!"

"Don't worry about that," Ross told him. "It'll throw the dogs off our scent."

Donnelly didn't have any trouble believing that. The stink from the bulb was so strong that his eyes were starting to water.

Ross finished smearing the liquid on the two of them, then wiped his hands on the grass. It was clear that he had more than a passing familiarity with the enigmas of the swamp.

"Come on..." he said to Donnelly, and the two men started moving again.

Chapter 47

Unsurprisingly, the pungent stink of the flower sufficed to throw the dogs off their trail as they continued traipsing through the swamp. After a while, however, Donnelly ceased to notice the smell, although he wasn't sure if that meant the scent had faded or he'd grown accustomed to it. Most likely the former, as Ross mentioned at one point that the plant's aroma was only a temporary reprieve.

"The flower can only mask us for so long," he admitted, "and those dogs are damn good trackers. Sooner or later, they'll pick up our scent again."

With that in mind, they had stayed on the move, although Ross remained cryptic about where they were actually going, saying only that they were headed for "shelter." Thus, they had been trudging along for an hour or two when Donnelly finally caught sight of what he assumed was their destination: a quaint, isolated cabin situated on a small parcel of land. As they drew near, Donnelly noticed a vast assortment of junk sitting on the porch of the cabin, as well as the small clearing that served as a yard. There were fishing poles, water jugs, a still, and an old cast-iron stove, among other things. There was also a rocking chair, currently occupied by Mama Lu, who sat there laughing to herself.

"What is this place?" Donnelly asked.

"Mama Lu's cabin," Ross replied. "This is where she's lived all these years."

"But where she'd get all this stuff?" Donnelly inquired, now realizing that there was even more miscellany than he'd initially noted.

"Local floods, capsized boats…" Ross explained. "Maybe she even steals some of it."

"Well, I'll overlook any infractions if she's got something to drink around here. I'm damn near dying of thirst."

"I think we can help you out," Ross told him.

He then walked towards the still, with Donnelly following him. Once they reached it, Ross grabbed a cup from a nearby bench that also held a couple of moonshine jugs; he placed the cup under the still's tap and turned it. The cup began to fill with a clear liquid, which Ross offered to his companion. Donnelly eyed it suspiciously for a moment, then down it in a single gulp. Immediately afterwards, a look of surprise came across his face.

"Mmmm," he droned. "That's actually pretty good. Is that what's in these?"

As he finished speaking, he grabbed one of the moonshine jugs from the bench and popped the cork out of it, preparing to drink. However, Ross snatched it away from before a single drop came out.

"I don't think you want to be drinking this one, friend," Ross stated as he took the cork and put in back in the jug.

Donnelly frowned. "Why not? Is it poison?"

Ross laughed. At the same time, he turned the jug around and showed Donnelly a small lizard painted on the side.

"No, it's not poison," he explained, "but it can get you killed."

"How so?"

"It's one of Mama Lu's concoctions: an aphrodisiac that draws reptiles for miles around. So unless you want snakes, alligators, and lizards following you around for the next two weeks, I'd suggest you leave this alone."

"So it's catnip for reptiles. What's she use it for?"

"Baiting traps."

"Traps?" Donnelly repeated, plainly befuddled. "So she catches snakes and lizards to keep as pets or something, like that baby gator she had before?"

Ross snickered. "You obviously have no appreciation for Louisiana cuisine."

Brow creased, Donnelly reflected on that for a moment – and then understanding dawned on him.

"Oh…" he muttered.

But before he could comment any further, a voice from the porch drew their attention.

"Hey, Ross," said a soft feminine voice. "It's about time you showed up."

Donnelly glanced towards the speaker and then stared: the person standing there was Susie Washburn.

Chapter 48

Susie looked much like her picture: young and pretty. At the same time, however, she exuded a solemnity that went beyond her years – a maturity that hadn't been present in the photo.

It might have been the result of living in the swamp for what Donnelly assumed had been months. That's obviously the type of thing that can make a person grow up pretty quickly. But in truth, he suspected that the air of adulthood around Susie had more to do with the baby that she currently held to her bosom – an infant she was breastfeeding at present.

Donnelly found himself hit by something of a double-whammy: first seeing Susie Washburn in the flesh, then noting the maternal act she was engaged in. Basically, with respect to the latter, it had been years since he'd seen a woman nurse a baby in public. The practice had been more prevalent when he was a kid, but had become less common in the intervening years. In fact, breastfeeding itself was on the wane. For instance, his own sister was using bottles and formula for her firstborn, despite the fact that she herself – like Donnelly and their other siblings – had been breastfed as infants.

That said, Donnelly was cognizant of the fact that breastfeeding was still the standard in many rural areas (and it didn't get more rural than Evangeline). Moreover, doing it in public clearly didn't garner the same level of stigma in rustic regions as it did in urban areas.

All of this zipped through Donnelly's head in just a second or two. Nevertheless, he seemed to have trouble processing everything he was seeing. Fortunately, Ross once again came to his rescue.

"Susie," Ross said, "I'd like you to meet the man who's going to help us. Agent Donnelly, this is Susie Washburn."

"Pleased to meet you, sir," Susie stated, extending a hand towards Donnelly while continuing to hold the baby with the other.

"Uh…likewise, I'm sure," Donnelly told her, finally finding his tongue as he shook the proffered hand. At the same time, he realized a couple of things.

First and foremost, Susie Washburn's initial comment about Ross finally showing up suggested that they – or at least Ross – had been expected. It also implied that Ross had known Susie was here…had probably known where she was all along. Ergo, the man had intentionally wasted Donnelly's time on multiple occasions.

Frowning, Donnelly turned towards him, but didn't get a chance to say anything as Ross began motioning everyone inside.

"We've got plans to make," Ross declared, "and not a whole lot of time, so let's get to it. Also, there are some things we need to clear up for Agent Donnelly."

That suited Donnelly just fine, as he had quite a lot on his mind at the moment. Presumably he'd get answers to the many questions that were now buzzing around in his brain. However, as they walked inside, he found himself staring at the child Susie held.

Judging solely from appearances and the way he was dressed. Donnelly assumed that the child was a boy. However, what drew his attention was the baby's complexion.

Although Ross and Jaspar had nearly identical pedigrees, their skin tones – as Donnelly had been given to understand – had been markedly different. Whereas Ross could easily pass for White, Jaspar had been conspicuously Black (or overtly biracial at the very least). To Donnelly, that suggested that the baby might have some telltale sign of his Negro blood, but in his opinion it wasn't evident in any discernable way.

"That skin color must run in your family, Ross," Donnelly noted after a few moments. "This baby doesn't look Black at all."

"That's because he ain't," Susie informed him.

"But…but…" Donnelly muttered, dumbfounded. "But I thought…I mean…"

"You figured this was Jaspar's baby?" Susie asked. "That he would be Black 'cause his daddy's Black? Well, Jaspar ain't my baby's daddy."

She paused for a moment, then went on. "Me and my baby, we got the *same* daddy…"

Chapter 49

Deputy Conners was walking through the swamp bent over, looking for tracks on the soggy ground. Like almost everyone else in their posse, he had spent a good portion of his time scouring the area for any sign of their quarry ever since the dogs had lost their scent. It was tedious work, but there was no way around it at the moment. Suddenly, however, he saw something that got him excited.

"Zeke!" he yelled. "Over here!"

Sheriff Washburn and Agent Kimble swiftly headed towards him, followed by everyone else.

Pointing at his find, Conners stated, "They left a footprint, Zeke. We got'em now!"

"Alright boys, let's go!" the sheriff ordered. "And unless they pick up the trail again, keep those damn dogs outta my way. They're damned near useless at the moment."

With that, the group set off through the swamp.

****

Ross and Donnelly were walking around Mama Lu's yard pulling a huge cart full of jugs, the contents of which they were emptying into the shape of a huge circle around the cabin.

"I can't help but feel sorry for her," Donnelly muttered softly, glancing towards the cabin as he emptied one of the jugs.

"Who, Susie?" asked Ross.

Donnelly nodded. "I can't begin to imagine what a nightmare this has been for her…everything she's gone through. I mean, I knew the sheriff was a hard man, but I never imagined him as a…"

"A monster?" Ross suggested as Donnelly trailed off. "He's not the first father to do something heinous to his daughter, and he won't be the last."

Donnelly simply nodded at this. He understood now why Sheriff Washburn hadn't seem to care if Susie was alive: he didn't want people finding out what he'd done. Even his bigoted and racist buddies wouldn't tolerate things like that.

Thankfully, Donnelly hadn't forced Susie to relive any of her ordeal by talking about it. Her statement about the baby had shed a light on almost everything. Instead, he had mostly listened as Ross laid out a makeshift plan to deal with the men pursuing them. It was risky and uncertain, to say the least, but they didn't have a lot of options. Shortly thereafter, he had found himself outside with Ross, hauling a cart of jugs around.

"But I still can't figure out why you didn't just come forward when we first got here," Donnelly admonished.

"If we had come forward with everything as soon as you arrived," Ross replied, "you'd have been gone within an hour, saying that the missing girl had been returned and that there was nothing left to investigate. Case closed. You wouldn't have believed the truth. Instead, you would have put Susie and the baby right back in the Sheriff's power, and you can guess what he would have done to keep his secret."

"Also," he continued, "I couldn't just let Jaspar die in vain...and neither could Susie. You see, they actually did love each other – not romantically, but as brother and sister. Jaspar gave his life to save her and her baby, and now she's willing to do whatever it takes to make his sacrifice worthwhile. It's what you'd expect a brother and sister to do for each other."

"So you sat on the truth as a way of getting us to investigate Jaspar's death, knowing we'd realize that was the key to finding Susie."

"Would you have bothered otherwise? I mean, what's another dead nigger, right?"

"I can't say that I like being manipulated," Donnelly retorted. "But I think I understand."

"I didn't really think of it as manipulation," Ross countered as he shook the last few drops out of one jug before grabbing another. "My plan was simply to convince you that there was more to this case than met the eye. So I spoon-fed you bits and pieces of the entire puzzle, giving you enough clues to piece everything together on your own. Things didn't go exactly according to plan, as you can see…" He paused for a moment, reflecting on the recent visit he'd received from the sheriff and his buddies (and how only a bunch of convincing half-truths had probably saved him from a lynching.) "…but I think we still have a shot."

Just as he finished speaking, a loud crack reverberated through the air like thunder – a sonorous booming that Donnelly immediately recognized as gunfire. Almost simultaneously, Ross yelped in agony, staggering forward as if shoved violently from behind. A moment later, blood began gushing from his shoulder. Ross looked at the wound in shock.

"I didn't mean a *literal* shot…" he mumbled.

Chapter 50

Ross began to fall forward, but Donnelly managed to catch him before he hit the ground. At the same time, more shots began to ring out, kicking up leaves and dirt at their feet as Donnelly hurriedly helped Ross back towards the cabin.

As they shambled forward, Donnelly glanced in the direction the shots were coming from. Although the sun had been burning off the morning fog, enough of it remained to make visibility something of an issue – especially beyond the clearing around the cabin. (At a guess, it seemed like the wind was blowing some of it in from more humid areas of the swamp.) That was both a blessing and a curse: it made it problematic to eyeball their attackers, but presumably made it difficult for those shooting to get a bead on them.

The first order of business, however, was to get to shelter – the cabin. As they lurched across the porch, Susie opened the door for them. They quickly staggered inside while Susie closed and barred the door. At that point, the shooting appeared to stop. Grateful for that small miracle, Donnelly gently lowered Ross to the floor, then ripped the shirt open to get a look at his injury.

"It's just a flesh wound," Donnelly announced. "Looks like the bullet went straight through. You'll be alright – assuming we can get you to a doctor."

"Mama Lu…can take care of me…" Ross said between deep, ragged breaths, "…better than any…backwoods sawbones."

As he spoke, his great-grandmother came and dropped to the floor beside him, gripping his hand. Apparently the injury to her last living relative had cut through the haze of senility and dementia that usually fogged her brain, because – in Donnelly's opinion – she looked completely sane and normal for the first since he'd met her.

He also noted that she had brought over what looked like a small, zippered pouch, which she quickly opened after releasing Ross's hand. Donnelly managed to catch a glimpse of some of its contents, including several needles and some small spools of thread. His first thought was that it was a sewing kit, but then he saw Mama Lu pull a vial of liquid from the pouch and pour it on Ross's wound. That's when he realized that the pouch wasn't meant for tailoring; it was a makeshift medical kit.

At that juncture, however, he had no further time to dwell on the subject as Susie called out to him.

"Agent Donnelly," she said, peeking out a window through some antiquated drapes.

He quickly stepped to her, noting that the baby was now resting peacefully in an old, rickety crib in a corner.

"What do you see?" he asked.

"Not a lot," she admitted. "The mist makes it a little hard, but there's about a dozen of them spread out behind the trees yonder."

Squinting, Donnelly peered in the direction indicated. He couldn't see anyone distinctly, but he could make out shadowed forms moving through the haze. He knew without a doubt that one of them was the sheriff. And another was surely his turncoat partner, Agent Kimble…

As if on cue, Sheriff Washburn's voice suddenly interrupted his thoughts.

"You in there, baby girl?" the sheriff shouted from cover of the trees.

Opening the window, Susie yelled out, "Yeah, I'm here, Daddy."

"Why don't you come on out?" Washburn asked.

"Why don't you go to hell?" his daughter retorted. "We both know that's where you belong."

Suddenly angry, the sheriff raised his rifle and began firing indiscriminately into the shack, with clear disregard in relation to who or what he might hit.

Chapter 51

Sheriff Washburn kept firing until he apparently ran out of bullets. At that point, a baby's crying could be heard coming from the cabin. Before the sheriff could reload, Kimble stepped towards him and grabbed the rifle.

"Hey, hey Zeke! Calm down!" he yelled. "Just calm down for a second. You keep that up and we won't get'em out alive."

"Who says we want to?" the sheriff demanded angrily.

Kimble looked at him in stunned surprise. "Zeke...she's your daughter."

Washburn blinked, as if this was news he was hearing for the first time. He then glanced at the others with them, noting several of them looking at him expectantly, then turned his attention back to Kimble.

"But you know what she did," the sheriff declared. "She shamed our whole family."

Kimble gave him a solemn nod. "Still, how about you let me try it my way?"

****

Inside the cabin, Donnelly took a swift look around as the gunfire outside came to an end. Everyone was understandably on the floor, a position they had all assumed as soon as bullets had started hitting the place. Susie had snatched the baby from the crib at the sound of the first shot, and now lay protectively on top of it. The child was wailing loudly, but neither mother nor child appeared to be injured.

Similar to Susie, Ross – flatly ignoring his injured shoulder – had somehow managed to place himself over Mama Lu and now shielded her with his body. However, neither seemed to have been hurt by the latest volley.

Agent Donnelly managed to take all of this in with a glance, as well as conclude that he himself hadn't been hit. However, that fact only offered small relief, as all of his instincts were now telling him that something was happening outside.

With that thought in mind, he quickly rose and – gun in hand – crept to the window, telling the others, "Stay down."

Peeking out, he saw Agent Kimble walking towards the cabin with both of his hands in the air, bent at the elbow.

"What do you see?" asked Susie.

"My partner," Donnelly added. "He's headed to the front door."

Before anyone could comment on what that might mean, Kimble spoke.

"Trevor?" he called out. "You in there?"

"I'm here," Donnelly yelled in response, "so just hold it right there."

Kimble complied, coming to a halt. "We need to talk, Trevor. You're making a mistake."

"My only mistake was letting them stick me with an asshole partner like you."

"Come on, kid. Let me in so we can talk. I'm unarmed."

There was silence for a moment; Kimble assumed that Donnelly was talking it over with the others in the cabin.

"Alright, you can come in," Donnelly said after a few seconds, "but you make one move other than what I tell you, you're going to find yourself missing some gray matter."

"Got it," Kimble said as he resumed walking towards the cabin, hands still raised.

Once he reached the porch, the door was cracked open slightly. A second later, the door opened wider and Kimble found himself staring at the barrel of a gun. At the same time, a hand suddenly grasped the front of his suit jacket and yanked him unceremoniously inside.

Kimble was unsurprised to find that it was his estranged partner who held the gun on him. Still keeping his hands up, he took a quick survey of the room while Donnelly – with gun still in hand – stepped to his rear and began patting him down, beginning at his armpits and working downward.

Kimble first saw Ross on the cabin floor with what looked like a gunshot wound to the shoulder. Next to him was Mama Lu, who seemed surprisingly calm. Finally, he noted a young woman, who was holding a baby with one hand while closing and barring the door he'd just come through with the other.

Recognizing her, Kimble said, "Susie Washburn, I presume."

Rather than speak, she simply gave him a curt nod in reply. Kimble was on the verge of asking about the baby she held, but never got a chance as Donnelly finished searching him.

"He's clean," Donnelly announced, stepping back in front of Kimble and once again pointing his gun at the man's face.

Kimble smiled. "Like I told you – I'm unarmed."

"Great, now what do you want?" Donnelly demanded.

"It's like I told you back at the hotel," Kimble said. "I'm on your side."

"Bullshit," Donnelly shot back. "I saw you at a Klan rally – wearing sheets, laughing, giving secret handshakes…"

"I told you before that I once hated Blacks, and I'm from the South as well. That being the case, joining the Klan was like a rite of passage for me…a natural stepping stone. But I told the truth when I said I don't think like that anymore, although what I learned back then has gotten us a lot of info on this investigation. But you've got to trust me."

"To hell with that!" Donnelly growled. "As far as I'm concerned, you're as bad as all those clowns outside, and I'm going to enjoy blowing your head off right now."

Kimble's eyebrows went up in surprise, as it looked like Donnelly was actually about to pull the trigger. Caught unprepared, the senior FBI agent suddenly found himself at a loss for words.

"Wait…" Ross muttered feebly.

Donnelly blinked, not sure he'd heard correctly. "What?" he said over his shoulder.

"Wait," Ross repeated. "I think…I think…we can…trust him."

Donnelly frowned but didn't respond. Instead, he looked at Susie, clearly soliciting her opinion.

In answer to Donnelly's unasked question, she stated, "I trust *Ross*. If he says we can trust this man, then I will."

Donnelly pursed his lips in anger, then let out a deep breath and muttered, "What the hell…" He then lowered his gun.

Kimble, showing obvious relief, slowly brought his hands down.

"You made the right decision, kid," Kimble told Donnelly. "I'm proud to be your partner. Really makes me hate what I have to say next..."

Recognizing that something was amiss, Donnelly suddenly realized that Kimble was holding a gun. It was a small revolver – so small that it almost looked like a toy in Kimble's hand – but a gun nonetheless, and it was pointed at *him*. Moreover, although his own weapon was in his hand, it was pointed down. There was no way he could raise it and get a shot off before Kimble plugged him.

Donnelly could have kicked himself, as he immediately realized what had happened. He had only searched his partner from the armpits down. Kimble, however, had apparently had the tiny gun up the sleeve of his jacket, and with his arms raised it had escaped both visual notice and Donnelly's search. Then, when Kimble lowered his hands, the gun had slid neatly into his waiting palm, allowing him to get the drop on his partner.

"Sorry folks," Kimble said with a grin, "but I'm afraid the only way any of you are walking out of here, is at gunpoint."

Chapter 52

Sheriff Washburn watched the cabin, growing noticeably impatient.

"How long's he been in there?" he asked no one in particular.

"'Bout ten minutes," Deputy Conners replied after glancing at his watch.

"Well, we're not gonna wait much longer," the sheriff declared. That said, he hadn't really come up with a solid method of dealing with the folks in the cabin.

Agent Kimble's idea of sticking a small gun up his sleeve had seemed ingenious. That should have given him an opportunity to catch Ross and the others off-guard. But considering how long he'd been inside, it seemed that either he hadn't had a chance to implement the plan or hadn't been able to pull it off.

Of course, they could always rush the place. However, although it was still somewhat misty, the clearing around the cabin had far less haze that the trees. Ergo, if they tried storming the front door, at some point they'd likely be easy targets – assuming, of course, that those scoundrels in the cabin had weapons. (As far as he knew, they hadn't yet returned any gunfire, but they could just be conserving their ammo.)

Another option was to surround the cabin, and – instead of storming the front door – try coming at them from all sides at once. They'd still have to cross the clearing, but that offered better odds than everyone rushing the front entrance. The real problem, however, was that gunplay was likely to break out, and with men on all sides, his group was bound to get hit by friendly crossfire.

Even worse, Washburn thought, *one of these fools might shoot* me.

All in all, rushing the cabin wasn't a viable plan. Given his druthers, the sheriff would have preferred to just shoot the place up – riddle it with bullets from top to bottom. That would take care of all his problems. (In particular, it would avoid the risk of his daughter saying some things that it wouldn't do to have others hear.)

Unfortunately, there were two FBI agents in there at the moment. One dead agent – specifically, that young shit Donnelly – he could handle, especially if the man's partner were available to back up any story about how he came to be deceased. Two dead agents, however, would invite further scrutiny and another investigation, and *that* Zeke Washburn didn't need.

Bearing all the facts in mind, it seemed that there was nothing to do at the moment but wait.

As the sheriff brooded, Conners suddenly began sniffing the air.

"Does something smell funny to you?" he asked a moment later.

"It's the fucking swamp," one of the other men replied. "Of course it smells."

"I know that, you asshole," Conners shot back, "but–"

Feeling something on his pants, the deputy stopped abruptly and looked down. There was a small lizard scampering up his leg. Several others were on his boots. Shouting indistinctly, Conners leaped to the side and began brushing the reptiles off with his hand.

"William, stop that crazy shit," the sheriff demanded.

"But Zeke," he pleaded, "there's lizards all over me."

The others with them suddenly began making similar comments.

"Now there's some on *me*," noted one.

"Me, too," declared another.

Much like the deputy, the others were now brushing the lizards off their clothes. All of a sudden, the bellow of a large alligator sounded nearby, causing everyone to go silent. Seconds later, another gator – seemingly closer than the first – answered with a cry of its own. Everyone began looking around nervously, trying to see through the mist.

"I don't like this, Zeke," Deputy Conners blurted out. "Something ain't right."

"That's for sure," the sheriff agreed, stomping on a lizard near his foot. "And we're not waiting any longer."

Chapter 53

Looking towards the cabin, Sheriff Washburn shouted, "My patience is startin' to wear thin! Y'all got exactly one minute to come out of there!"

There was no response for a moment, then Agent Kimble shouted from the window, saying "It's alright. I'm bringing them out, but Ross is hurt and the baby's being fussy."

Seconds later, the door to the cabin opened. Ross came out first, helped by Donnelly. Ross had his left arm draped over Donnelly's shoulder, while Donnelly's right arm was around Ross's back, with his right hand just below Ross's armpit. They were followed by Susie, who was carrying the baby, and finally Mama Lu. Kimble brought up the rear, covering the others with his gun.

The group trudged despondently across the clearing, coming to a stop about a dozen feet from Sheriff Washburn, who had stepped out from the cover of the trees. Likewise, the sheriff's cohorts had also come into view, forming a loose semicircle around the party from the cabin. Still keeping his gun on them, Kimble walked forward, taking a position next to the sheriff.

"Any problems?" Washburn asked.

"Not really," Kimble answered. "Like I told you, the kid here" – he gestured in Donnelly's direction – "is still too green to be a good agent."

"You bastard!" Donnelly growled at Kimble. "I can't believe you're helping these animals."

Deputy Conners snickered. "I think you got it backwards, boy. *You* the one helpin' the animals, siding with niggers instead of your own kind."

"Well, at least they don't rape their own daughters!" Donnelly shot back.

All of a sudden, everyone went silent, and more than a few of those in the sheriff's posse appeared stunned by what they had heard.

"Wha...what?" muttered Conners.

"Didn't you know?" Donnelly responded. "Jaspar never got Susie pregnant – *he* did!"

As he finished speaking, he pointed accusingly at the sheriff.

Deputy Conners looked at the sheriff in shock. "Zeke?"

"He's lying," Sheriff Washburn stated flatly. "Kill him."

Nobody moved. Taking advantage of the confusion, Susie spoke up.

"It's true," she declared. "He beat me when I tried to fight him off and threatened to kill me if I told anybody. Then he spread the lie that he was just trying to keep me in line because of Jaspar."

Under his breath, one of the men with the sheriff's posse – Riley – muttered, "It can't be…"

"Think about it," Ross suddenly said, speaking with more force than he seemed capable of. "Would any of you let a man – let alone a nigger – keep working at your home if you thought he was sleeping with your daughter? And Jaspar worked there almost up until the time they ran away."

The members of the sheriff's posse exchanged glances, but no one said anything. After a few seconds, Conners looked at the sheriff.

"Zeke, is it true?" he asked. "They telling the truth?"

"Susie was showing up black-and-blue long before the sheriff hired Jaspar," Ross continued. "He wasn't the reason Sheriff Washburn raised a hand to his daughter. The sheriff had a different reason for doing that."

Washburn looked dumbfounded – plainly unsure of what to say next. All of the men who had been willing to follow him through the gates of hell just minutes ago were suddenly looking at him with something akin to distaste. It was one thing to put uppity niggers in their place (especially those with the gall to chase White women) or to protect one of their own from high-handed revenuers. It was something else entirely to shield someone who had violated their own child, and – showing a level of humanity that they had lacked thus far – even the sheriff's cronies seemingly had a problem with that.

However, everyone's attention was suddenly drawn to the dogs as they unexpectedly began whining. The animals had been generally quiet up to that point, but almost simultaneously they began acting agitated and making sounds of distress.

The distraction caused by the canines seemed to bring the sheriff back to himself.

"That's it!" He barked, glaring at Ross. "You're dead, nigger!"

Still scowling at Ross, he shouted, "Riley!" There was no immediate response, prompting him to shout again a few seconds later. "*Riley*!"

"Um…yeah, Zeke?" Riley mumbled, seemingly unsure of himself.

"Shot this nigger," the sheriff ordered.

Riley, who was standing just a few feet from Washburn, looked anxiously from the sheriff to Ross, then back again. "Uh, Zeke…"

Sheriff Washburn suddenly took a step in his direction and grabbed Riley, pulling him close.

"Did you hear what I said?!" Washburn shouted in the man's face. "I said shoot him! Now do it!"

He then pushed Riley away, shoving him in the direction of Ross and Donnelly. Nervously, Riley raised his rifle and pointed it directly at Ross's chest. Ross, still supported by Donnelly (who, surprisingly, didn't move away), looked Riley directly in the eye without flinching. A moment later, a shot rang out.

Simultaneous with the gunfire, Riley appeared to jerk slightly. A look of confusion settled on his face and then he looked down at his chest, where a spot of blood had appeared and was now swiftly spreading outward across his shirt. A moment later, he fell face-forward onto the ground, dead.

"What the hell?" mumbled Conners, openly dumbfounded (like most of his compatriots) concerning what had just happened to Riley.

He looked around in befuddlement for a moment, and that's when he saw it: a glint of metal in the underarm portion of Ross's shirt, where Donnelly's hand was positioned to allegedly help support the injured man.

Chapter 54

Suddenly, Donnelly let Ross slide gently to the ground, thereby revealing a gun in his right hand that he aimed generally in the direction of a couple of their adversaries. He counted himself fortunate in that Riley's compatriots hadn't immediately responded to his shot by opening fire. Presumably, they had been under the impression that the gunfire was from Riley shooting Ross as ordered. Riley falling down dead, among other things, had clearly shown that to be a faulty assumption. However, before anyone could react, Kimble unexpectedly stepped close to Sheriff Washburn and shoved his own weapon into the sheriff's side.

"Eh?" Washburn muttered in surprise. "What's this?"

"Sorry, Zeke ole boy," Kimble told him, "but I guess you got the wool pulled over your eyes on this one."

He then shouted to the rest of the sheriff's posse, saying, "Alright, all of you drop your weapons, or the sheriff gets it."

As he finished speaking, he gave Donnelly a surreptitious nod, mentally patting himself on the back for how quickly they had come up with a workable scheme.

****

Frankly speaking, it had been something of an audacious plan. It had come together when Kimble – after surprising everyone in the cabin by pulling a gun out of his sleeve – had stunned them all a second time by turning the weapon over.

"Maybe now you'll believe me when I say I'm on your side," he had told Donnelly while handing him the firearm.

Needless to say, it had been a convincing display of trust, and enough to win the confidence of his partner and the others. Kimble had then swiftly explained how he'd attempted to use his Klansman background to try to get information from Washburn and his buddies. He hadn't been able to find out much, but had managed to persuade them all that he was "one of them." More to the point, he had played the role to the hilt (including wearing some borrowed Klan regalia), which had ultimately led them all – in part – to their current predicament.

With respect to how to escape this particular dilemma, Kimble had told them bluntly, "The sheriff seems pretty indifferent to any of you leaving the swamp alive."

At that juncture, Susie had told him the truth about her baby, causing him to revise his opinion and declare, "In that case, he most *definitely* will not let any of you leave the swamp alive. He might even kill me if he thinks I know something."

Kimble had then reiterated his earlier statement: that Donnelly and the others leave the cabin at gunpoint.

"If I act like you're my prisoners and walk you out," he explained, "that'll buy some time…and maybe a chance to keep everybody from getting killed."

"What's to keep the sheriff and his lackeys from just shooting us as soon as we set foot out the door?" Donnelly had inquired.

"What do you think I've been doing when I sneak out every night – playing bingo?" Kimble shot back. "I've been getting to know the sheriff…getting close to him and his Klansmen buddies. I've met men like him before and I know his type. If he thinks you're my prisoners, he's not going to shoot you – at least not right away. He's going to want to gloat first."

"He's right," Susie agreed. "When my daddy thinks he's got you cornered, he loves to rub it in."

"That means his guard…will be down," Ross added, breathing heavily. "Question is how do we…take advantage of that?"

They had quickly brainstormed on it, and in less than a minute came up with the notion of Donnelly sneakily holding a gun while pretending to help Ross walk.

"That still only leaves us with two guns against a party of armed men," Kimble stated when they were done strategizing. "Not great odds."

"Well, we did have a *separate* plan," Donnelly admitted. "Something we were working on when you and your new friends made an appearance."

He then swiftly explained to his partner the scheme that he and Ross had been implementing when Agent Kimble and the others had shown up. When he was done, Kimble just stared at him, almost stupefied.

"Well, I wish I could say I've heard worse plans, but I'd be lying," Kimble admitted. "That has to be the craziest thing I've ever–"

At that point, he was abruptly cut off by Sheriff Washburn, shouting from outside that he was out of patience.

"I guess it's showtime," Kimble announced, then headed to the window and yelled that they were coming out.

Minutes later, they were all outside, Riley was dead, and Kimble had a gun on the sheriff. But – perhaps most importantly – everyone knew what the sheriff had done to his own child.

Chapter 55

With an armed Agent Donnelly in front of him and Kimble poking a gun in his ribs, it didn't take the sheriff long to figure out that the tables had turned to some degree.

Glaring at Kimble, he hissed, "You nigger-loving bastard!"

"Sticks and stones," Kimble stated with a smile as he disarmed Washburn with his free hand and tossed the weapons aside. "Sticks and stones…"

He then shouted again to the rest of the sheriff's troop, saying, "I said to drop your weapons. I won't ask again."

The sheriff's fellow Klansmen all hesitated, glancing at each other anxiously, trying to decide what to do. In Kimble's opinion, this had always been the riskiest part of the plan (not counting the crazy, *separate* plan Donnelly had mentioned). Basically, Washburn's posse had them outmanned and outgunned, but Kimble and his companions had been operating under the theory that if you cut off the head, the body will die. Or rather, if you can *control* the head (i.e., Sheriff Washburn) then you can *control* the body (his sycophants). The fact that nobody was moving to obey Kimble, despite the threat to their leader, suggested that maybe the revelation about the sheriff and Susie had backfired to a certain extent. Maybe they didn't view Washburn as their leader anymore…

Kimble decided to test that hypothesis by poking the sheriff harder with his gun, making him grunt audibly.

Apparently understanding what was required of him, Washburn said, "Do what he says, boys."

However, he almost had to shout to make himself heard above the dogs, who were not only starting to bay loudly, but were also straining at their leashes in an effort to get away. The man handling them – a reed-thin fellow with a bushy, unkempt beard who was holding a rifle – struggled to keep them under control.

The sheriff's posse continued to look unsure of themselves for a moment, but then one by one they began dropping their guns as commanded. Kimble felt tension he hadn't been aware of leave his body, and he relaxed slightly. It was looking like he, Donnelly, and the others just might make it through this thing alive. And then pandemonium broke out.

It began with the dogs. They were already barking and baying, while moving back and forth in obvious agitation. The man who held their leashes was one of the last to put his weapon down, but just when he dropped his rifle as ordered he unexpectedly cried out in pain. A moment later, he was hopping around on one foot, with the other leg raised.

Looking at the man, Donnelly saw what initially appeared to be some kind of vine attached to his calf. A moment later, he realized what he was looking at.

Snake! he belted out mentally.

At the same time, one of Washburn's posse yelled, "That's a cottonmouth!"

Donnelly wasn't familiar with snake breeds by sight, but he knew many of them by reputation. Thus, he was well aware of the fact that cottonmouths were venomous, with a bite that could be fatal.

At that moment, the snake seemingly let go, and dropped to the ground. It swiftly slithered away, with folks leaping wildly to get out of its path. In fact, watching the cottonmouth weave its way across the clearing, it became evident that there were numerous snakes on the ground, as well as a number of lizards.

"What the hell is going on here?" muttered Conners.

It was obviously a rhetorical question, but it wasn't clear whether anyone heard him over the dogs. When their handler had gotten bitten, he'd let go of their leashes, and the hounds were now dashing madly about the clearing, barking and yapping loudly.

All of a sudden, however, the hounds scattered wildly, running in terror. A moment later, the reason why became clear as a huge gator rushed into the clearing. Faster that Donnelly would have thought possible, it dashed forward, snatched one of the dogs in its mouth, and then kept going until it disappeared into the trees and mist on the other side of the clearing.

"Holy shit!" Kimble blurted out. Like his partner, he had been watching everything unfold but could barely believe his eyes. He'd always thought of gators as slow and lumbering; he had no idea they could run so fast. Moreover, from the time the dog's handler had gotten bitten until the gator ran through and grabbed a meal, no more than ten or fifteen seconds had passed.

All of a sudden, another of Sheriff Washburn's cronies – a man dressed in blue overalls – rushed towards the dog handler, who had just collapsed to the ground. Producing a long knife from somewhere on his person, the fellow in overalls sliced open the leg of the dog handler's pants at the spot where he'd been bitten; a second later he put his mouth to the man's leg, as if kissing it. A moment later, the man turned his head to the side and spat, making it clear what he was doing: attempting to suck the poison out.

As the fellow in overalls continued dealing with the snakebite, Donnelly found himself dwelling on the blade the man had produced. It suddenly made him cognizant of the fact that quite a few of sheriff's posse probably had knives on them. (In particular, he recalled that Deputy Conners kept a blade in his boot.) In short, they had gotten their adversaries to drop their guns, but hadn't truly disarmed them. That meant the men around him and his companions still represented a clear and present danger, and – with the advantage of numbers – they were sure to try something. At the moment, however, almost everyone appeared mesmerized by what was happening with the snakebite victim.

The guy wearing overalls suddenly stopped his ministrations. At that moment Donnelly noted two things: first, the leg that had been bitten was starting to look incredibly swollen and discolored. Second, the dog handler himself appeared to be unconscious…or worse.

"He's gone, Jimmy Joe," one of the other Klansmen said to the fellow in overalls.

"You take that back, Clem!" Jimmy Joe shouted at the speaker. "My brother ain't dead!"

"Well, if he ain't," Clem – the speaker – responded, "he gone lose that leg."

Scowling, Jimmy Joe suddenly appeared to get a tighter grip on his knife. Frankly speaking, it looked like he was about to attack Clem.

Without warning, the roar of a gator sounded from just beyond the trees, capturing everyone's attention and seemingly making Jimmy Joe forget his anger. The beast was answered by one of its fellows on the other side of the clearing. And then by a third.

"Oh, damn!" exclaimed one of the Klansmen, looking around anxiously. "We're in some type of gator feeding ground."

There was silence for a moment as those words sank in, and then Ross spoke.

"That's right," he said, sitting up. "Mama Lu thinks of the gators around here as pets. She throws her scraps and leftovers into the yard here, and they come eat it up. She also brings back anything she finds in the swamp that they might eat and leaves it out for them: dead animals, half-eaten carcasses, roadkill… With gators always around here, people stay away. It's part of the reason almost no one's been able to find out where she lives all these years."

Washburn and his men listened to this in stunned silence, with several of them suddenly looking like they'd prefer to be elsewhere – and with good reason. Feeding an alligator was about the worst thing you could do in the swamp. Gators were normally leery of people and avoided them. But when folks started feeding them, gators would lose their natural wariness of human beings. Even worse, they would tend to start associating people with food, and that always ended badly.

In short, if Ross was telling the truth, they were all in serious danger. As if to emphasize that point, a nearby gator abruptly let out a sonorous bellow, so loud and disconcerting that everyone looked in that direction.

Sensing that Kimble was distracted by the alligator, Washburn unexpectedly hammered an elbow into his stomach. The force of the blow knocked the wind out of Kimble, and he went down on all fours, coughing violently. The sheriff took off running, moving faster than most would have given him credit for as he headed for the trees and went dashing through the swamp. Donnelly fired at him as he ran, but missed. Struggling to his feet, Kimble drew in a deep, painful breath and – gun still in hand – went after Washburn.

Chapter 56

Sheriff Washburn wasn't the only one who took advantage of the distraction caused by the reptiles to make his escape. Several of his fellow Klansmen took the opportunity to flee as well. A few, however – including Deputy Conners – chose instead to try retrieving the guns they had dropped. Turning his attention from the fleeing sheriff, Donnelly shot two of them without hesitation and then dove aside as Conners, who had managed to recover his own weapon, fired at him.

The bullet hit him in the leg and Donnelly grabbed the limb, moaning in pain. At the same time, he found himself facing another obstacle: lizards and snakes, which began swarming over and around him. Almost terrified that one of the reptiles might have a poisonous bite, he began brushing them off in a nigh-panic.

Sensing that he had an advantage, Conners ran towards Donnelly, ready to fire again. Ross, forgotten and lying on the ground (where he had stretched out once gunplay began), swung out a leg, tripping him. The deputy went sprawling, but before he could get up Ross leaped on his back, punching him in the side with his good arm.

"Take *that*!" Ross yelled as he struck Conners. "And *that*!"

Deputy Conners bucked wildly, throwing Ross off. He then dove on top on Ross, who had landed on his back, and began pummeling his injured shoulder. Ross wailed in agony.

"Felt that, did ya?" Conners snarled between blows. "Well, it's nothing compared to what I did to that jungle-bunny cousin of yours!"

He then pointed his gun at Ross's forehead.

"I'd love to give you the same treatment I gave Jaspar," he continued with a malicious grin, "but I ain't got the time to–"

Deputy Conners stopped abruptly as an alligator rushed into the clearing from the nearby trees, hissing angrily. Swiftly – almost instinctively – he pointed his gun at the animal and fired several rounds. At least two appeared to hit the gator, which roared in pain and scrambled back towards the trees

Recognizing that he had a small window of opportunity, Ross suddenly brought up his good arm, holding a bunch of moist swamp muck in his hand. He swiftly smeared it across Conners's eyes before shoving the deputy off him. Conners fell to the side, screaming and rubbing his eyes vigorously.

"My eyes!" he howled. "My eyes!"

Struggling to his knees but obviously unable to see, he began firing wildly in what he took to be the spot where Ross lay. Ross, however, had already scrambled away and his shots went wild (although one almost hit Donnelly, who – heedless of reptiles and his injured leg – scuttled backwards to get out of the line of fire).

The deputy kept shooting until his gun was empty. By that time, Ross had managed to slip behind him. Then, as if he'd been waiting for this moment his entire life, Ross hooked his good arm around the deputy's throat and began squeezing as hard as possible.

"This is for Jaspar," Ross declared forcefully, "you White piece of shit!"

The deputy began to struggle wildly – clawing madly at the arm that held him and trying to punch Ross in the face. It was all wasted effort, as none of it made Ross loosen his grip in the slightest. He continued choking until

Conners went limp. At that point, Ross released his hold and the deputy slumped over. Breathing hard, Ross then noticed Agent Donnelly limping towards him.

On his feet after managing to avoid getting shot or bit, Donnelly shambled forward until he was next to Ross and looked down at Conners's body.

"He's dead," Donnelly commented casually.

"Yeah," Ross admitted, although Donnelly had undoubtedly seen the entire episode. "I guess you're angry that I killed one of your suspects."

"No," Donnelly answered, shaking his head. "I'm just upset that *I* didn't get to do it. Glad to see that you're okay, though."

"Thanks," Ross said as Donnelly reached out a hand and helped haul him to his feet.

Following this Donnelly spent a moment looking around, then asked, "Where's Susie?"

"Huh?" asked Ross, frowning.

Both men scanned the area in bewilderment. Aside from the bodies of dead Klansmen, the only person in sight was Mama Lu. She had apparently meandered back to her rocking chair on the cabin porch during all the ruckus, and now sat there, rocking and chuckling softly to herself.

Susie and her baby, however, were nowhere to be seen.

Chapter 57

Sheriff Washburn ran pell-mell through the swamp. Not far behind him was Agent Kimble, furiously intent on catching up as the morning sun burned off more of the surrounding mist. Unfortunately, he found himself distracted by several gators heading for the clearing as he ran, and as a result he lost sight of his quarry.

Breathing hard, Kimble stopped in a small glade and looked around. He hadn't been that far behind, so the sheriff had to be close by. Catching movement out of the corner of his eye, he took off in that direction. However, he was just passing a tree when Washburn, hiding on the other side, struck him brutally across the chest with a broken tree limb. Kimble staggered backwards then went down hard onto his back.

Stepping into view, Washburn kissed the tree limb.

"Hot damn!" he exclaimed, striding towards Kimble. "I tell ya, when you find a proven method of doing business, it always pays to stick with it."

Now standing over Kimble, he raised the tree limb and struck down with it. Agent Kimble, in obvious pain, managed to avoid the blow by rolling to the side. Scrambling to his feet, he raised his gun hand towards the sheriff…only to realize that there was no gun in it. Understanding that he must have lost it when he fell, he scanned the ground anxiously and quickly spotted it nearby.

Unfortunately, the sheriff saw the gun as well, and both men went for it at the same time. As luck would have it, Kimble got to it first, but as he reached for it Washburn struck his forearm with the tree branch he still gripped.

Letting out a sharp cry of pain, Kimble yanked his arm back.

"Smarts, don't it?" Sheriff Washburn stated with malicious glee. "Well, it's gonna get a lot worse before it's all over."

"Then maybe you should just give up now," Kimble said snarkily.

The sheriff laughed, then rushed at Kimble. Swinging his makeshift club methodically back and forth in front of him, he slowly made his opponent retreat until Kimble backed up against a tree.

Kimble ducked a blow that came close to taking his head off; it landed with a solid thud on the tree. Seeing an opening, he swiftly stepped inside the sheriff's guard and threw two solid punches to Washburn's stomach. The sheriff doubled over, and Kimble used the opportunity to kick him in the jaw. The blow sent the sheriff sprawling onto his back.

Kimble rapidly closed in, but Sheriff Washburn kicked out unexpectedly, striking Kimble's knee and wrenching it to the side. Kimble grunted in pain, at the same time going down to one knee. The sheriff then raised up and swung the branch, striking Kimble on the head. Kimble pitched over, semiconscious.

Washburn got to his feet and staggered over to the gun. After picking it up, he strolled back and aimed directly at Kimble's head. Kimble, now fully conscious, merely stared down the barrel of the firearm.

"I guess you win," he told the sheriff.

"Like I told ya before, there's a higher law than man's," Washburn said. "Now you pay the price for your ignorance."

A gunshot rang out then, followed swiftly by another. Kimble shuddered with each one, but was surprised to find he hadn't been hit. Slowly, Sheriff Washburn lowered the gun and turned around. Behind him, Kimble now saw Susie, still holding the baby and a gun – presumably a firearm that had been dropped by one of Washburn's group. A wisp of smoke was coming from the just-fired weapon in her hand. He also noted two bullet holes in the sheriff's back, which were now weeping blood.

For a moment, Sheriff Washburn just stared at his daughter and the baby (who – despite the noise from the gun – was not crying), then he reached over his shoulder with one hand and touched his back. A second later he brought the hand back in front of him; it was covered with blood. Washburn simply gazed at it for a moment, then started laughing.

He was still laughing seconds later when he slumped to his knees. At that juncture, Susie came forward and pointed the gun right between his eyes. Her father looked at her and laughed even louder.

"I guess you're more like your old man than I thought," he snickered. "You're as much a killer as I am…"

****

Ross and Donnelly were hustling through the swamp, doing their best to follow what Ross had determined was Susie's trail. Traveling at good speed despite their wounds, they came to a sudden halt upon hear a gunshot. Anxious now, they began moving even faster.

"Billy!" Donnelly called out. "Susie!"

"Trevor!" Kimble yelled in response. "Over here!"

The two men followed the sound of Kimble's voice and soon came upon him sitting on a fallen log. Nearby, Susie was standing over the body of her father, who now had a bullet hole in his forehead. She still held the gun in one hand and her baby in the other. Ross tried to take the weapon from her, but Susie – almost in a stupor, refused to let go.

"It's over, Susie," Ross assured her. "It's over. Let go."

She turned to look at Ross. There was still a blank expression on her face, but this time she didn't resist when he tried to take the gun from her. Meanwhile, Donnelly helped his partner up, who still seemed a bit woozy from the blow he'd taken to the head.

"You okay?" Donnelly asked.

"I'll be fine," Kimble insisted. "You?"

Donnelly pointed to his leg, which now had his belt wrapped around the wound to stop the bleeding. "Never better."

They both began laughing.

"So I guess our plan wasn't so crazy after all," Donnelly suggested, still snickering.

"What, using some weird elixir to attract a bunch of swamp critters?" Kimble said. "It sounds crazier every time I think about it."

"Well, at least it wasn't really a feeding ground," Donnelly noted, reflecting on that part of their scheme.

The "feeding ground" narrative, of course, had been an on-the-spot fabrication by Ross. The real reason the alligators (and all the other reptiles) had been drawn to the area was because of Mama Lu's "reptile catnip," as Donnelly had previously referred to it. He and Ross had been in the process of spreading it around the cabin when the latter got shot.

In essence, they had known that the sheriff and his cohorts would eventually catch up to them. Ergo, their stratagem had been to make a stand in the cabin and allow the advancing reptile horde – particularly the gators – to drive off Washburn and his fellow Klansmen. Kimble turning out to be on their side had given them more options, but ultimately they had still needed to rely on their "crazy" plan to some extent. (For instance, Ross would surely have gotten his head blown off had they not implemented this particular scheme.)

"Anyway," Kimble droned, bringing Donnelly back to himself, "it's over now. Let's get a move on."

"Sounds good to me," Donnelly told him. Turning to Ross and Susie, he asked, "Any objection to getting out of here?"

"None whatsoever," Ross replied as he put his good arm around Susie and the baby. He then began gentle urging Susie forward as they all began walking out of the swamp.

Chapter 58

Two weeks after their escapades in the swamp, Kimble and Donnelly sat in David Stanford's office, waiting patiently while he read the report of their investigation. After what seemed like a lifetime, Stanford let out a deep breath, shaking his head in disbelief as he closed the file folder.

"Well," he said, "this has got to be the most bizarre report I've ever read. Not to mention the most sordid…" Frowning, he drummed his fingers on his desk for a moment. "The girl?"

"She took her baby and left town," Kimble stated. "The rumors about her and Jaspar would have made it impossible for her to live there."

"And the truth would probably have made it worse," Donnelly added.

"What about this Ross Johnson?" Stanford asked. "Do we need to have another conversation with him?"

"I don't think so," Donnelly answered, "but it would probably be difficult."

Stanford gave him a curious look. "Why's that?"

"Because he left Evangeline as well," Donnelly replied.

"But there's really nothing else to talk to him about anyway," Kimble offered. "All he did was provide some helpful information. It's all in the report."

"So why did he find it necessary to hightail it out of town?" Stanford inquired. "I mean, I understand why the girl wants to get the hell out of Dodge, but why *him*?"

"Because snitches end up in shallow graves, Dave," Kimble declared. "Almost nobody wanted to help us, and by telling us *anything* this man put his life in danger. That's all he did, but there are people in that town who will kill him for it. So yeah, he left."

As he finished speaking, he shared a knowing glance with his partner. In short, the essential portions of their report were true, but a lot of it was bullshit – particularly where Ross was concerned. In short, the two agents knew that many folks – including people in their own agency – wouldn't brook a Black man killing someone White, no matter how justified it might be. Ergo, they had changed a lot of the details (such as Ross choking Conners to death).

In essence, as they had walked out of the swamp with Ross and Susie, the four had collaborated on the story they would tell. Much of it dealt with explaining dead bodies, but those could be classified as justified shootings by the agents or the result of friendly fire. It also didn't hurt that it took several days to get assistance from other law enforcement agencies. Ergo, by the time Donnelly and Kimble were able to lead a contingent of peace officers back to Mama Lu's cabin (with Ross's help, of course), it was practically impossible to determine anyone's cause of death because most of the bodies were too badly decomposed, chewed up by swamp denizens, or – as in the case of Sheriff Washburn – just flat-out missing. (Personally, Donnelly believed Ross might have played a role in regard to some of that, but kept those thoughts to himself.)

Of course, there was always a chance of someone coming forward with a different version of events – specifically, those Klansmen who had been in Washburn's posse and then run off when things went sideways. However, if they ever tried to tell what really happened, they'd have to admit to being part of what was basically a lynch mob. That's probably why, despite currently being in custody, none of them were talking.

Thinking of the men in question, Donnelly asked, "So what's happening with the rest of those who were helping Washburn?"

"We're still holding them," Stanford replied, "applying pressure and trying to get them to crack. But they're staying tightlipped – probably because they know a conviction isn't likely."

"Why the hell not?" Donnelly demanded. "Kimble identified them all as being part of the sheriff's posse."

"Yeah," Stanford agreed with a nod, "but their lawyers are saying every man in that group was deputized by Sheriff Washburn, so they believed were operating under authority of law."

"And even if that wasn't the case," Kimble added, "every one of them will probably have ten witnesses willing to stand up in court and say that they were somewhere else when all that shit was happening in the swamp. Believe me…I've seen it happen."

"Come on," Donnelly countered. "They can't stand before a judge and argue that they were there acting as deputies, and at the same time say they were somewhere else entirely."

"Actually, they don't have to say anything at all," Stanford insisted. "Remember, people have a right against self-incrimination, so none of these men have to take the stand, even in their own defense."

"In other words, their lawyers will put on evidence that they were never in that 'gator feeding ground,'" Donnelly surmised, employing a term he and Kimble had used in their report. "And if they *were* there, it was under the belief that their actions were sanctioned."

"And don't forget that it was a nigger that they were allegedly after," Kimble added. "No jury in Louisiana is going to convict them for that."

"But they also shot at two federal agents," Donnely protested.

"Revenuers," Stanford corrected. "The argument will be that they shot at revenuers."

"Huh?" Donnelly muttered. "Revenuers deal with laws and revenue related to alcohol. That's not *us*."

"As far as many people are concerned, *every* federal agent is a revenuer," Kimble noted. "And revenuers, in general, are hated far and wide."

Donnelly, sat quietly for a moment. "So you're telling me that the rest of the sheriff's cronies will go free."

"Probably," Stanford admitted, "but that doesn't mean you two didn't do a great job. And, while I'm not trying to take credit for it, you two actually made a pretty good team."

"Yeah," Kimble confirmed with a nod, then grinned at his partner. "I mean, despite being green and untested in the field, the kid did alright."

Donnelly chuckled. "And notwithstanding the fact that he's over the hill and uses archaic methods of investigation, the old-timer didn't do too badly either."

"Old-timer?" Kimble echoed with a laugh, to which Donnelly merely shrugged, continuing to snicker.

"Great," Stanford said as he reached into his desk drawer and pulled out a file. "Now that we're all comfortable with the working relationship, here's your next case…"

THE END

Thank you for purchasing this book! If you enjoyed it, please feel free to leave a review on the site from which it was purchased.

Also, if you would like to be notified when I release new books, please subscribe to my mailing list via the following link: http://eepurl.com/ginmVT

Finally, for those who may be interested, I have included my blog info:

Blog: https://hercsamsonbooks.blogspot.com/

Made in the USA
Thornton, CO
10/22/24 13:34:17

ae33efec-52d1-4c42-a299-fbcce3912428R01